Deep Hunting,
Shallow Fishing

Deep Hunting, Shallow Fishing

Stories by William Mills

CHRONICLES PRESS
ROCKFORD, ILLINOIS
2006

for Aimée and Sarah
and once again their mother

Dwight Browne and Stephanie Foley deserve special thanks
for their help with the creation of this book.

Contents

Other Books by William Mills

POETRY

Watch for the Fox
Stained Glass
The Meaning of Coyotes

FICTION

I Know a Place: Stories
Those Who Blink: A Novel
Properties of Blood: Stories

CRITICISM

The Stillness in Moving Things: The World of Howard Nemerov
John William Corrington: Southern Man of Letters

NON-FICTION

Bears and Men: A Gathering (Text & Photographs)
The Arkansas: An American River (Text & Photographs)
Louisiana Cajuns (Introductory Text)
Images of Kansas City (Photo Selection & Introduction)
Black Sea Sketches (Text & Photographs)

Deep Hunting,
Shallow Fishing

The Electric Duck and
the Camouflaged Woman

S kipper McCauley's vision came when he was waiting for his step-daughter-in-law, Debbie Dell, to come in on the Greyhound Bus. He picked up an old copy of *Ducks Unlimited* and noticed that fellows were making big bucks taking out-of-towners hunting in the woods-styled "Green Timber Hunts." There were small classified ads in the back of the magazine, and two of them concerned hunting lodges just ten miles from where he worked as a farmhand in northeast Arkansas. He was staggered by the fee the lodges charged.

Soon his brain was on fire counting the money he was going to make with his own lodge and wasn't paying attention when Debbie Dell got off the bus. Skipper didn't want to think about Debbie Dell because she only reminded him of the general fix he was in and had been in.

Debbie Dell, a plump sixteen, had permitted Skipper's fifteen-year-old stepson Elvis to have his way with her and soon announced that the additional ten pounds she had put on recently was Elvis' doings. Skipper couldn't see what the boy could have seen in her. Now, Debbie Dell stayed home all day at Skipper's watching TV. Skipper had not greeted this new mouth to feed with good humor and now there was a general sullenness on Debbie Dell's countenance which soon caught on with Elvis. Elvis sulled up even more when Skipper told him to find work. This was why Skipper had been at the bus station—Elvis was stocking shelves at the Jitney Jungle.

With his mind on the vast sums of money coming from his hunting lodge, Skipper was startled when someone standing right in front of him blocked out the light. Not only wide-bodied Debbie Dell but a huge stuffed dog she had both arms around.

"I'm here."

"I reckon you are. The driver charge extra for that dog?"

Debbie Dell's brow furrowed, then she mumbled, "I dunno. Mama bought the ticket."

Skipper wasted no time the next day. Duck season wasn't far off. He drove his rusting farm truck over to Randolph Barrow's even before the landowner had finished his morning coffee and biscuits.

"You up bright and early, Skipper."

He went straight to the point. "I got a new idea how we can make some money."

"Always interested in money. Sit down, sit down," bringing his coffee out on the porch. "What's gotcha all excited?" Randolph liked Skipper. He was a cut above the average tractor driver or farm manager. He could even carry on a conversation which the landowner didn't get much of. Randolph had inherited 5,000 acres of rich rice and soybean land and overseeing that was all he managed to do. Never left the county. When Skipper showed up, offering to be farm manager, Randolph listened to his proposition and hired him. Skipper got a run-down house over by the Current River and the use of an old truck.

Skipper had been in the used-car business over in Memphis and he claimed the stress of the job drove him out of city life. Now he was looking for peace and quiet. It had come to Randolph's attention later that Skipper's stress may have come from getting out of Tennessee one step ahead of the law and the motor-vehicle division. It seems Skipper was handy with tools but even handier with vehicle identification numbers. By the time Randolph came to this knowledge, he had grown attached to his employee, especially since now Randolph seldom had to go to the fields.

"Ducks."

Randolph was mystified. "Ducks?"

"Ducks and duck hunters. We need to start a huntin' lodge."

Randolph thought a bit. "I think a huntin' lodge would cost a lot of money and I ain't investing in no hunting lodge."

Skipper knew Randolph had tons of money in certificates of deposit at the bank in Pocahontas, because one day Randolph had gone into a tizzy about a quarter-percent decline in interest.

"Won't have to. They can stay at my house. Whatcha think of that?"

"I know you got a nice house" (he knew it wasn't, it was beat up and had a leaking roof which Skipper had mentioned more than once), "but you think you got enough extra room with all them kids you got?"

"During duck season, I'll move 'em all into one room."

Randolph Barrow looked off in the distance for some time while he thought this over. "I dunno. I got all I can handle around here. I don't know much about duck hunting. I shot two one time on the pond back of the house, but that's about all."

"I'll take care of everything. All you got to do is let me flood some of those rice fields that run through that patch of woods near the river. You know, after the combine gone through. We'll have ducks grandma. Besides, you'll like having new people to talk to."

"Well, go ahead, I guess, long as you're going to take care of it. I got my plate full."

"Nothin' to it. Winter's slow anyway. Whatcha say we just split the profit right down the middle?"

"What will these boys pay?"

"Three hundred dollars a head."

Randolph whistled.

"I saw such in a magazine. There'll be some expenses. Magazine ads. Probably need some decoys. Course that includes room and meals. But what the heck, Merlee is a good cook."

"That she is." When Randolph's family drove him up the walls he exited "to talk over business" at Skipper's and sometimes he was there at supper time.

Next morning Skipper was dead set on driving over to Sikeston to a famous hunting and fishing store where he knew he could buy some decoys. He had a few from when he used to hunt near Memphis on the Mississippi, but not nearly enough for a lodge. He asked his other stepson, Maynard, if he wouldn't run the tractor in his place at least for the morning. Maynard said he would, being brighter than his brother Elvis. He had figured out getting along with his stepfather had more advantages than not.

"I got to finish up some before dark," Maynard commented. "Cherry and I are going out to check deer sign."

"Shore." Skipper knew Maynard liked nothing better than deer hunting. The boy hunted every day of the season. Skipper could understand that boy. . . Elvis he couldn't. Besides, Cherry Flashpole was a good-looking little thing, came from a good family over at Outer Imboden. Skipper decided Cherry might be the reason Maynard was still in school. Whatever worked. He knew it wasn't just deer sign they were checking.

An hour after breakfast the next morning he was walking into the Fin & Feather. The owner was a good ol' boy from Sikeston who had parlayed his little bait shop into big business. Skipper had talked to him briefly when he stopped in to buy some tackle. He was in the store when he got there.

"Need a bunch of decoys."

"Just so happens I have several thousand."

"Don't need all of 'em. Maybe five dozen."

"A special on six."

"Give me six. I'm going into the duck-lodge business."

"Do tell."

"Yeah. Randolph Barrow and I gon' be partners."

The owner knew Randolph Barrow, knew he had the money and the land. He also figured what kind of partner Skipper was. The one that did the work. As the two men began to stuff the dozens of decoys in net sacks, the merchant said, "If you're going into the professional guiding business, you got to have this latest decoy. It'll drag a mallard right out of the sky." He held up one for Skipper.

"Strangest looking decoy I ever saw. Ain't what you call right light either."

"That's cause this here decoy runs off batteries. Here, lemme show you." He attached the wires of the battery to a tiny motor inside the duck and held it up on a metal rod. All of a sudden the duck's wings began to whirl around.

Skipper stared for a minute, then said, "That's the damnedest thing I ever saw. An electric duck."

"Fellow shouldn't even go on the water without one of these. You know how skittish these ducks get by the time every farmer and his brother in Canada and the Dakotas done shot at 'em. Anything look like a normal decoy spread, they look down from a thousand feet and keep on going. Can't get their attention. They see this, they'll land in your lap."

"How much are these a dozen?"

"A dozen? You don't need a dozen. Just one, maybe two."

"How much is one of 'em?"

"Two hundred dollars."

"Jezus. For a electric duck. Think I'll pass."

Before Skipper could get out of the store, the merchant stopped by the display of duck calls.

"You seen the Duck Killer's new mallard call? Try it out."

Skipper put it to his lips and suddenly blew a hailing call that scared a woman customer out of her wits.

"Oh my lord."

"He's trying it out, ma'am."

"I just came in for some bobbers for my husband. Didn't know I was going to go deaf doing his shopping."

Skipper began a chuckling feeding call, then a mournful come-back, comeback call, and as the woman started for the entrance he ripped off his hailing call again.

As she bolted out the door the merchant said, "I believe you know how to blow that thing."

"My daddy taught me. He's dead now."

Before Skipper left with his six-dozen decoys in the back of his truck, he had bought a Duck Killer's call.

Over the next few days he was brimming with confidence about the coming season and was already silently counting his money.

Shoot, he thought, why not offer goose hunting, too. He had a buddy in central Arkansas who kept telling him he had thousands and thousands of geese—Canadas, snows, and speckled bellies—all eating up his crops. Thus goose hunting was included in the ads he ran.

Still, there was this nagging sense of inadequacy when the subject of the electric duck came up. Worse, one of his competitors, Myrl Wilhoit, had been demonstrating it at the filling station. True, some of the fellows got a laugh out of it, seeing the duck's white metal arms swinging in a circle, but Myrl allowed that he had already tried it out before the season started, and it worked like a magnet.

The pressure became so intense that Skipper was going to have one even though he didn't have the two hundred dollars. He was going to make his own. After all, the duck itself was just a regular decoy that had been hollowed out. Inside, there was a little motor that ran off batteries. Where would he get this motor? Beads of sweat broke out on his forehead with all his pondering until, hallelujah, he raced over to an old VCR that the kids had mishandled. Soon he had the small electric motor out and jammed up the duck's backside. Then all there was to do was mount the duck on a four-foot piece of half-inch reinforcing bar left over from a building project. Skipper hooked up the wires from the little motor to the tractor battery, and behold, the little wooden arms he had whittled and attached to the motor began to rotate.

Debbie Dell came out the back door, stopped, and stared at the whirling machine. "What's that?"

"An electric duck."

"Oh," with no wonder in her eyes, only suspicion.

Just then Elvis slouched out of the house and stood by her.

"He said it's an electric duck."

"I already seen one. Myrl Wilhoit got one. 'Cept his is new looking."

Skipper said nothing.

"You reckon you could make a goose?"

"I guess I could if I wanted to."

"Wilhoit got one."

That did it. Skipper was not going to be bested. He had the goose decoy, but what about a little motor? His brain's circuits began to pop and flash, then a solution. Soon he was working on a backup combine. It had a lot of wear, but in case the newer one broke down during harvest, Randolph Barrow had this one. Except Skipper was now taking a small electric motor out of it.

The small motor was a little heavy for the project at hand, but he'd make it work. Later when he had hollowed out the goose, installed the motor, and mounted it on the rebar, he noticed it had a tendency to fall over. He'd figure that out later.

While the family was finishing what was left of a last year's deer roast, the phone rang and Debbie Dell went over to the kitchen counter and answered it with her sullen "hullo," expecting Elvis from the Jitney Jungle.

"What?" Her plump face became wrinkled with confusion. "Green Timber Lodge? No you got the wrong number," and hung up.

"Wait, wait, that's for me." yelled Skipper, too late.

"He wanted the Green Timber Lodge," she mumbled.

"That's us."

Debbie Dell did not answer, just frowned and went back to hacking a piece of the venison roast.

"That could've been my first piece of business!"

"You didn't tell us we were the Green Timber Lodge, Skipper," said his wife.

"Well, you got to fancy things up." He brooded for a moment and when the phone rang again he leaped at it. "Hello . . . yep, it sure is. How can I help you?" He listened for a few moments, then, "We got ducks everywhere . . . covering the sky . . . in the creeks, in the rice-fields. How many of you? Two's fine. Get lots of personal attention. Uhuh. Flying all the way from Boston . . . do tell! Yeah, there's an airfield over to Jonesboro. Sure, we'll pick you up."

As he hung up he gave out a "Yeeehaaa. Our first customers."

"When they coming?" asked Merlee, warily.

"This weekend."

"You know I got to grocery shop 'fore they come. That's gonna cost extra money. Have to buy some steak or something fancy."

"You know, Merlee, I think they'd be interested in eating our own good country cookin'. Grits and ham for breakfast, a good chunk of deer meat for supper. I bet they don't even have deer meat in Boston."

"If you say so. It's your deal."

The next evening new customers and new complications. Two fellows wanted to go goose hunting at the same time the first party was hunting greenheads. When Skipper quickly multiplied $300 times four hunters, he agreed. But he knew the goose hunting was twenty miles away on his buddy's place. His friend said the Snows and the Canadas were eating his crops down. That meant he had to get some help. He would have to run the goose hunt. Maybe he could rope in Randolph. He'd have to give him a quick duck-calling lesson or two. After all, he was getting half the money. Course he had the land . . . and the woods . . . and the ricefields. Old Smokey, his Lab retriever would work for Randolph. He'd work for anybody.

Back on Randolph's porch next morning Skipper explained the new situation. "We're catching fire with this hunting lodge."

"Are, huh?"

He told him about a fully booked weekend, but also the dilemma of needing another guide. Matters fell silent for a moment with no help from Randolph Barrow. Then Skipper told him what he had in mind.

"Me. Shit, I know next to nothing about duck hunting. I already told you that."

"Ain't nothing to it. I show you what pit you all will hunt out of and you can have ol' Smokey." There was a pause. "They'll bring in six hundred bucks. For maybe four hours work. Nothing to it. I'll show you how to call 'em in." Skipper pulled out his Duck Killer call.

"Hold off, there. My wife'll run both of us off you start wailing away with that."

"Come down to the house before supper. It won't take thirty minutes. We'll fry up some catfish."

That cinched the deal. About an hour before sundown Skipper had Randolph Barrow blowing a duck call for the first time in his life and sounding very much like a chicken in its last moment of life trying to outrun a pickup on the blacktop. Secretly Skipper had many doubts but the brand-new Green Timber Lodge was under pressure.

Just before being called in to supper, Maynard and Cherry Flashpole drove up to this concerto for mallards. Both were dressed in camouflage. Cherry was fitted out for her own kind of hunting. She had on the tightest pair of hunting pants and knit jersey that had ever graced the woods around Pocahontas or Outer Imboden.

"Here, let me," taking the call from Randolph. She proceeded to run through the repertoire, from quiet desultory "quacks," to a chuckling feeding call, a mating call, a piercing hail call, then a pleading comeback, the diaphragm of her chest swelling in the light of the back porch lights.

"Shuckins, where in the world did you learn that?" said the astonished Randolph.

"At phys ed in Imboden," she replied, leaving Randolph shaking his head.

"Soup's on," yelled Merlee out the back door.

The Green Timber Lodge's battle plan was put into effect by Skipper before he left to pick up his two hunters in Jonesboro, making at least two of his personnel very unhappy. Elvis and Debbie Dell were informed that Maynard was to bunk with them while the clients were there. If Debbie Dell was sullen before, she could step on her lower lip after the announcement.

Skipper had no trouble recognizing the guests at the little airport. The two men had brand-new duffle bags, brand-new hunting clothes, and expensive gun cases. One of them easily tipped the scales at three hundred pounds. He turned out to be a German.

Skipper greeted the men in the tiny building that called itself a terminal dressed like he always was dressed, wearing his camo ball cap and camo fatigue pants. He worked on the farm dressed that way year-round. His clients were a great contrast in full Orvis regalia

"Mr. Cabot?"

Mr. Cabot strained to look at him. "McCauley?" He seemed suspicious.

"Welcome to Arkansas." He shook Cabot's hand.

The fat man offered his hand saying only, "Schroeder."

Cabot's Boston reserve could barely hide his disdain when he saw Skipper's truck. Skipper, who had carried their bags while they carried their gun cases, heaved the bags in the truck bed behind the cab.

"Is there room for our guns in the cab?"

Skipper took off his cap and scratched his head a second. "Might be kind of tight."

"These are Bernellis."

"I'll try to drive careful," he answered, full of sincerity.

It was clear the only place for Cabot was riding between Skipper and the German. Schroeder would never have gotten his fat thighs around the floor shift.

Shortly after they were under way, Skipper learned that Cabot was "in faucets." Brass faucets among other things.

"Mr. Schroeder makes the machines that I use in my factory."

"*Ja.*"

Soon Skipper learned how many hunting lodges Cabot had been to in Canada, North and South Dakota, right on down the Mississippi River flyway and finally at the Hackberry Rod & Gun Club in Hackberry, Louisiana. Somehow he had missed Arkansas, but now he was going to remedy that, after which he would work on the Pacific flyway.

"Now you said there were plenty ducks, right?"

"Yes, indeed. Geese, too. The place you'll be taken to in the morning may have both."

"*Gut, gut,*" remarked Herr Schroeder as he took a flask from his hunting coat and downed a slug. In the close cab the air became incendiary. He offered the flask to Cabot, who politely declined.

Skipper, sensing that Cabot was uneasy, began to call attention to better points of rice-field country though without much luck. Skipper hadn't expected this part of the job, entertaining strangers.

Suddenly Herr Schroeder, who was feeling quite ebullient, saw a late afternoon sky covered with thousands of geese. "*Gott!* Look!"

Even Cabot relaxed at the sight, although he did point out that he had seen even more than this in Manitoba and Louisiana.

In the final light of the day as Skipper neared his home county and the Green Timber Lodge, an eight-point buck broke across the road, setting off another explosive "*Gott!*" from Herr Schroeder. He was now a happy camper and whipped out his flask to take another swig.

"If it suits you fellows, we were planning on having deer meat for supper tonight."

Schroeder looked quizzical. Cabot said, "Venison."

"Ah, *das Wildbret. Gut, gut. Alles gut.*"

"You have that in Germany?"

"Oh, *ja. Die gute* restaurants all have it." Skipper was a little disappointed to hear this.

"You can't buy it in Arkansas. If you want it, you have to kill it yourself."

Eventually Skipper turned off the gravel road onto a very rough and, due to a recent rain, muddy road. His ancient truck flexed with the terrain like some beast accustomed to the effort all except for one hole that tossed Cabot to the roof. Soon Skipper brought the beast to a halt and opened his door. Schroeder opened his door and rolled his rotundity to the ground.

Cabot didn't move for a moment. He peered at the rusting roof of the house, the sagging porch, then looked askance at Skipper.

"Is this the lodge?"

"Yes, indeed. Green Timber Lodge. Here, let me get your bags."

In truth, Skipper's house was like numerous personalities in this region of the country, consciously rough, even crude on the outside, but inside, a bit better. After all, the house wasn't theirs, but the furniture inside was theirs. It was true that the bedroom where Skipper dumped their bags was filled with discount store furniture, but the living room-kitchen had knotty pine walls, and furthermore, the walls, although not possessing any pictures, were covered with deer heads, deer antlers, and stuffed ducks. There was even a "breakfast bar." And it was from behind this bar that a smiling Merlee held out her hand, although a bit tentatively.

"Welcome."

"How do you do, Thaddeus Cabot," stiffly.

Herr Schroeder pumped her hand vigorously. "Schroeder."

"Please have a seat. What can I get you to drink?"

"Do you have a beer?" from Schroeder.

Cabot pursed his lips briefly. "A glass of wine, perhaps."

Merlee looked at Skipper in a panic.

"I believe we're out of wine right now, but we do have a bottle of good bourbon," said Skipper to the rescue.

"Perhaps just a little."

The men had no sooner taken a seat and sipped their drinks when Debbie Dell waddled into the room with not a word to anyone and flopped on her spot of the sofa where she commanded the television.

"This is our daughter-in-law," explained Merlee, which secretly pained Skipper to admit, especially to his visitors.

"Hullo," she mumbled.

"Mr. Schroeder is from Germany," said Skipper to Merlee.

"Goodness."

Just then Randolph Barrow came in from the back porch. After more introductions, Barrow admitted he would take a little bourbon if there was any. Within a couple of minutes, despite Barrow's accent, Cabot felt he was more around his class. Soon enough these men were talking about money: interest rates, the Dow and for the only time in the evening Herr Schroeder was briefly troubled about the falling mark. This was dispelled when Barrow volunteered Skipper's bourbon for the German machine-tool maker.

"Ahh," he remarked with satisfaction after one sip, then took a bigger one. "*Wunderbar.*"

Adding to the company came Maynard and Cherry Flashpole. It wasn't long before Cherry was pumping her crossed, camouflaged legs from the stool of the breakfast bar and the machine-tool maker was keeping Skipper busy filling his guest's glass with his newfound discovery, American bourbon.

Soon Merlee was not only serving up a venison roast, but duck breasts wrapped in bacon. During this feast, Skipper explained that Barrow would be going with them to their shooting pit in the morning, while Skipper took care of goose hunters some twenty miles away. For a moment, a shadow passed over Cabot's face, when Barrow said, "You know Cherry, you ought to come with us in the morning, good as you are on that duck call. You, too, Maynard."

A very disappointed Maynard said, "I got to work in the morning."

"Well, what about it, Cherry?"

"*Ja, ja,* my dear, you must," urged the tool maker.

"I don't mind, if it's all right with Maynard." What could Maynard say?

"Take that electric goose, Randolph," offered Skipper. "We're just going to lie down in field where we're going. Won't need it. I'll be back after lunch and we'll all make a late evening hunt, too."

So it was that at four the next morning, the faucet maker, the tool maker, the rice farmer, the faithful Labrador, and Miss Cherry Flashpole were standing in a concrete pit covered with willow branches, looking out over water two feet deep at a couple of dozen decoys, plus, not only a homemade electric duck, but an electric goose, too, the latter two spinning their white wings in the early light.

No clarinet or harmonica player ever worked as intensely, as movingly as Cherry, filling her lungs time and again, sending out her hailing call, pleading with high-flying little vees and big vees of wild birds, coaxing them to join their robotic kinsmen below. And some did. The Bernellis fired again and again whereupon the faithful Labrador splashed out and returned with the crumpled flyers, earning the several hundred pounds of dogfood he ate during the rest of the year.

Of course, the dog could not straighten up the top-heavy electric goose decoy, and occasionally, first Randolph Barrow, and then even Miss Flashpole waded out, stood it up, and returned. After the second dead duck shot by the toolmaker, he commenced to toast them with his flask now filled with his new American companion, Kentucky bourbon. Which no doubt warmed his insides, even his soul, but did not improve his aim. *Machts nicht.*

The electric goose took a farewell dive and for the last time, Miss Cherry Flashpole, out of young deference to the much older rice farmer, waded out to straighten the goose. At which time the tool maker laid his Bernelli with some force on the concrete wall of the pit and it discharged. The number four shots ripped the surface of the water and soaked, with mud and muddy water, Miss Flashpole.

"Jesus," she screamed. "You could've killed me you sonofabitch." As one would expect, Miss Flashpole had inherited the tendency in this part of the country wherein her outside demeanor could camouflage another quite different person.

The little dynamo was running straight for the pit. She jumped down inside and the German toolmaker, full of drunken pity for himself, but also for Cherry, lamented "My darling . . . oh my *schatz,* I'm so sorry" and reached out to envelope her in his arms. As she jerked herself away she left half her tight jersey in his hand. All stood amazed at her heaving chest.

Skipper McCauley was home early. He was feeling expansive, for his goose hunters had limited out in an hour and he had pocketed the crisp hundred dollar bills. They had even tipped him. No question, things were looking up. As he looked out, he could barely see what looked like his other hunting party. Walking toward him. Even at a distance there was something that made him uneasy, sensing the apocalypse.

In amazement, he soon could make out Cherry Flashpole, naked from the waist up, holding a shotgun on Mr. Thaddeus Cabot and Herr Schroeder, cursing as she walked through the uneven field, as Randolph Barrow was heard to say, "Calm down, Cherry, it's all right."

Crabbing

Miami had been good to me for a time. I hid among the Cubans for several years. My marriage had broken up when I got back from Nam. Neither of us intended it, but I couldn't seem to hold myself, or us, together. Truth was I was bored with civilian life. I talked to a buddy or two who had been in the Drang and they felt bored too sometimes, but they hung on until the cadence of days quieted things down, drank beer and watched TV.

I drank too much, got mad at my wife too much, and finally she had too much. So I went south.

Being on the street in Miami made me think something was going on. It wasn't, but I thought so. The Latin record stores played loud beating music for the whole neighborhood to hear whether it liked it or not and many of the women moved and dressed like they were wooing the whole street. A little bit it reminded me of the one time I had a pass for Saigon, but only a little bit. The color, the movement.

I was broke a lot and I did what a lot of people who are broke do. I sat in the park in the sun. Here I sometimes ran into a guy who was abandoned at the Bay of Pigs. We had some things in common. I think I felt abandoned in some ways. Abandonment is a long story.

The Cuban wanted to return to his country. I sure didn't want to return to the Drang. That's a long story, too. In the meantime the Cuban picked up work where he could and when there was enough work, he brought me along.

Miami wasn't just full of Cubans. Lots of other people from the south. Mexicans, Salvadorans, Guatemalans . . . you name it. One day we were working on a construction job pouring concrete and I started talking to a Guatemalan kid. He was the only one of the three of them who could speak a little English. He said after this job he had found them work on a crab boat over on the Gulf Coast. That evening I was sipping a cool suds in the park and thought, "It might be a good idea to get out of Miami for a while. I wasn't making any headway. And crabbing sounded like it was just the ticket." Next day I asked him if the captain might need another hand.

A week later I had taken up life on the Island. The one drawback about this job was getting to the boat at three o'clock in the morning. Several days before I started to work, I spent the evenings at what was called the Oarhouse, the owner's attempt at a little humor. Fried fish in the front and cold beer and pool tables in the back. The back was where some of the crabbers hung out. It was there I had overheard these two Cubans asking about a boat that was missing. They had enough gold chains around their necks they would have sunk if they had been in the water. Turned out the father and brother of the Cubans were on a shrimper last seen near Marco Island. Several days later the Oarhouse bartender told me the bodies had washed up toward Key West. He remarked they may have been carrying more than shrimp. Right off I thought of all those gold chains. Didn't seem to fit the dress code of shrimpers. I never understood people who peddled dope or used dope dressing so anyone looking at them thought, "Doper!" Course we didn't have to worry about that in Nam because our employers picked out our clothes for us. Also didn't have to worry about where we would get our dope either.

I hadn't spent much time around salt water and my first morning out everything was new. Even though it was summer it was chilly that early in the morning and the air very fresh. There was almost a full moon when we started out and later after the sun broke the horizon, both of them were in the sky for several hours. The Gulf was green at first and only later turned deep blue.

I had eaten blue crabs before, but never heard of stone crabs, much less anything about catching them. Two of the Guatemalan kids had done this kind of work before and they worked hard and fast. The captain, an amiable nordic type who had worked his way down from Minnesota, helped break me in, too. Around twenty or thirty miles offshore he started looking for his marker buoy, one that had been registered with the state. Then all the fun began.

One kid was all the way on the starboard and one on the port. Each had a wooden pole six or seven feet long with a big hook on the end. As the captain maneuvered down the buoy line, one of them would reach over the side and grab the line attached to the buoy, take a few turns about a small hydraulic wench and let it bring up the trap to the side. Then the trap was hauled by hand over the side and dumped in a tub. The traps looked like oversize milk crates. Sometimes a trap was full, a lot of times nothing. Then traps had to be rebaited, often with pieces of stingray or pork skin and thrown back overboard. The third man, besides cutting up bait, had to break the claws off and throw the live crabs back into the sea. If he was in doubt about the minimum size of the claws, he had to measure them before breaking them off. The crabs, once they got to the bottom again, had to start over growing their claws back. A good thing for the crabber, tough for the crab. That's the trouble being the one eaten rather than the eater.

When a day working on a crab boat is over, you are happy to fix something to eat, catch an hour of TV, then hit the sack. I stayed with the Guatemalans in a trailer the captain provided for them. They were good kids, older than they looked, but there was an innocence about them that made them seem like children. None of them drank alcohol. They saved their money for their families back in the village in the mountains of their country. Me, I wasn't saving for anything. After I toughened up to the work, I didn't need as much rest, so I drifted down to the Oarhouse in the evenings. The kids might walk along for a short while, but then they stopped to buy sodas and candy and sensibly went back to the trailer.

I didn't have much in common with the pool players and most of the time watched a moving beer sign that seemed as good as most TV. One night a guy on the next barstool struck up a conversation and it turned out he had been in Nam, too. Different times, different outfit. We made very little talk about Nam, but it was a connection. After he left, I got to remembering things.

When my outfit came out of the field, we lived in barracks. Hot showers, hot food. We even had people to clean up our areas. We paid them out of our magnificent wages. I had a young Vietnamese boy who had lost both his parents in the war and he didn't seem to have any relatives around the base. He cried when I left. It wasn't the money—I fixed him up with somebody else. I had my mind on going home, getting out of the shit. I didn't realize home wasn't what I thought it was. I even started remembering a few good times in Nam, like soldiers will do. Guess it's the way the mind does tricks like that to keep the circuits from breaking down. A guy in our platoon said there was a Polish saying, if it hurts too much, forget it.

The captain had a little book that he wrote down where all his crab lines were and when he had run them. He tried to run each line once a week. Some of them were far offshore and he liked to do those when the tides and winds were right; otherwise, not only did it take longer to get there and return, but it took a lot more fuel.

One morning we were going to the most distant lines. Below the wheelhouse was a tiny crew quarters which was almost level with the main deck. The kids killed the time going out down there. I shot the shit with the captain and stayed out of the cold night air. Just as our little bit of the world was turning itself toward the sun, the kids started shouting over the diesels and waving their arms. One of them came tearing up the ladder and in a mix of excited spanglish made us to understand there was someone calling out in the water. Well, the captain thought they were nuts. We were fifty-five nautical miles from shore and he could see nothing. The kid insisted.

The captain, still skeptical, swung the boat slowly around, and all three of the kids were on the bow looking hard. And what do you know? They began pointing off to port and there in the water hanging on to a life ring was someone.

"Jesus! What is the guy doing out here?"

I sure didn't know. With the boat now almost dead in the water, I dropped down the ladder and leaned over to the side with the kids. One of them turned his gaft around and held out the end for the guy to grab. At first he didn't want to give up his life ring, but finally we got it, then him aboard.

He looked a mess. A drowned rat. His flesh was all wrinkled and white from being in the water a long time. The kids started jabbering away in Spanish. The little man who came out of the sea started jabbering in something else . . . almost none of it English. He was Oriental, you could tell that, and even with him speaking fast, bowing sometimes, shivering all the time, the words sounded familiar to me, like from a long time ago. "*Cam on that nhieu. Cam on that nhieu.*" He said this many times, bowing with his hands together in front of him. Lo and behold, he was Vietnamese!

I looked up at the wheelhouse and the captain had stepped out on the small runway. "Captain, you're not going to believe this, but this guy is Vietnamese."

"You shit."

Somehow between us all we figured out that he had been on a shrimp trawler out of Tampa. But that was about all we could figure out. Plus, he had been in the water a long time.

"I got to notify the Coast Guard," said the captain, and went back in the wheelhouse and worked the radio. In a few minutes, he came back out. "They are some pissed off at the shrimper. He never reported a man overboard or missing. He's already halfway to Key West. But they have turned his ass around and he's heading back. They also laid the law down to me that I'm to confine this dude anyway I need to. Put him in leg irons, or bind him some kind of way. He's not to get away, as they put it."

"You gonna tie him up?"

"Naw. He doesn't look bad to me. I don't get why he was out there, though."

We had not been able to understand him enough to know why he was in the water. That was a big mystery. If somebody had wanted him dead, he wouldn't have thrown him a life ring. Without that he would have been dead long ago. On the other hand, what would have caused him to jump that far out to sea?

I went back to the main deck and tried to use what little Vietnamese I could remember. He hung on to any words I managed to come up with.

"Viet Nam, o dau?"

He lit up. "An Khe."

I let him know I knew An Khe. He seemed happy enough with that. He didn't need me to tell him I had been there in the Army. An Khe wasn't much but I wouldn't have told him even if I had had enough Vietnamese. Still, hearing the sounds of his language sent me over the water again, back to the Ia Drang and I didn't want to go. Just sitting on deck, worn out from trying to speak a language I didn't know, I went back whether I wanted to or not.

Dog Co., First Platoon was the first out the door of the slick, the M60 trying to cut all the foliage away, plus all the gooks, when we came into the hot *LZ*. It was hot for another platoon already there, already getting cut to pieces, and surrounded. Here come more black horses of 1st Cav.

Charlie let us know he knew where we were with mortars. Each squad dug in or got behind what it could. Lt. Carroll, a fresh lieutenant from St. Louis couldn't call in supporting artillery because he didn't know precisely where the platoon was. Artillery is like sky diving, there is only an "A" grade or an "F."

O'Donnel from the next squad down was screaming he'd already been hit. There went the medic crawling through some grass to see what he could do.

By now Charlie's rockets were spreading shrapnel everywhere. Ted from our squad thought he was safe behind a big anthill. He wasn't. I was down behind a little berm, not much protection, but I could see his fatigue pants were stained with lots of blood. He had a terrible wound. He called out for me to help him. The way was all in the open but his screams left me nothing else to do. It was a crap shoot, but I made it. I cut his fatigue off the thigh that was cocked funny. Clearly it was broken and he was losing blood big time. Just then our sergeant ordered us to attack on our flank. I knew we had to do something, we couldn't stay here and get cut to pieces. The gooks knew exactly where we were now.

"Don't leave me, man. You know what they'll do"

Indeed, we all did. Charlie didn't take prisoners. They shot the wounded.

"I'll come back. Don't worry. We got to shut down their shit first so the choppers can get in. You'll get the first free ride," making a clumsy joke. "I'll be back, Ted. Scout's honor."

Our whole platoon started attacking the tree line where the shit was coming from. One of our guys killed two who were up in the trees. But then we hit the wall. Must have been a whole battalion. We had stepped into deep doo-doo.

Once the commander in a chopper overhead could see what we were into, he ordered us to move laterally to what he hoped was a possible landing zone where we could be extracted. Air Cav, right. I knew we were getting farther and farther from where Ted lay, his life leaking away. I screamed something to our sergeant over the roar of the firing, but he just gave me a shake of the head. Too hot. Sorry. Maybe he'll make it by hiding.

He didn't. He was abandoned.

We lost more guys before we were lifted out. I got a scratch in my shoulder from shrapnel but those who could walk, manned a corner of a poncho, carrying the badly wounded to the *LZ*. I made it on board, but with a few minutes to think, I was already feeling lousy about Ted.

Two things about that Polish proverb: Sometimes even if you want to forget what hurts you can't. Second, somehow you don't want to forget. Like you would be worse off because you would be ashamed before yourself. Still, it's between a rock and a hard spot, isn't it?

Which brings me back to the young man who came out of the sea. Either he was pushed or he jumped, I figured. The captain joked in the wheelhouse that the guy might have discovered the hoary naval tradition that it was his night in the barrel. Or he learned something he shouldn't have. Although he was in his late twenties, he seemed innocent. One thing for sure, abandonment will kill innocence every time.

Now Nemesis is making her way on board the shrimper. Matters had not been sorted out between the Coast Guard and the shrimper. Our captain was to bind him, but then what? Turn him over to the boat where this malfeasance occurred? And what had occurred? I studied his chapped, peeling face and dark eyes to see whether he was nervous about the approaching shrimper. Had its captain convinced the Coast Guard that it was all the Vietnamese's fault? Would the captain, who was American, escape the law of the sea merely because he spoke the same language as the Coast Guard? The law of the sea seems to exist in its own separate world, held together by tight customs and rigorous law. A captain, who is absolute master of the universe of his boat, can at times act like a father. What kind of captain is master of the shrimper? What will be the fate of our orphan?

Our boat was not running hard south using lots of our fuel to meet the shrimper coming from Key West. Our captain knew he wasn't going to be reimbursed for the rescue, so he idled along.

The captain said, "Try to tell your friend that he doesn't have to go on that shrimper if he thinks something bad is going to happen. I'll tell the Coast Guard we will fix it so he can't go anywhere and they can come get him.

Secretly I was happy that he said this; he wasn't going to throw him to the dogs, if they were dogs. Then I tried to get the message across to the Vietnamese. He nodded his head like he understood there was a choice, or it seemed he did. Without language, though, all you could do was watch the person's gestures. The face can send a lot of signals, much less with the hands.

The shrimper came in sight around a long cay, and soon was coming alongside. It was a bigger boat than ours and with two- or three-foot waves we had to move carefully to tie up briefly. The shrimper was a dirty boat, always a bad sign. Two deckhands who were throwing a hawser to us looked very red-eyed, not from being in the sun, and little doubt from amphetamines.

Our captain didn't leave his wheelhouse, but shouted or talked over the radio to the other captain. The shrimper said he never missed this crewman. Our captain wanted to get away and asked me what the kid had decided.

"You don't have to go," I whispered to him, but the kid answered quietly by climbing over the side to the other boat. It wasn't like he was going to his own people, or going home—he had no home. It was like he felt fated and sentenced to this life he had not chosen, but that his abandonment, his being thrown mercilessly into the world, was something he was going desperately to carry out.

He managed to say thank you in English as the shrimper cut loose. I watched it for a long time until it seemed to be nothing, but I knew it still was something. The captain happened to say, "They're going back to Key West. They've got some work to do on the boat down there for several weeks."

I knew what I had to do when we docked. I had to go to Key West.

Wildcat Roping

I moved to the Louisiana boondocks when my grandfather left me his little pea patch farm. I was only a year out of the Army and after playing soldier for two years, I thought I would play cowboy. Coincidentally I met an older fellow who had also played with guns and even at the age of forty-five he was playing cowboy himself.

My playing with guns had been under government supervision. The other fellow, Jake Knight, did his gun thing more under government surveillance, or at least that was what the government tried to do. Knight was an "international organizer" for the Teamsters, which I came to know was a "motivator" for the union. Guns, dynamite, and general mayhem in case the managers of a company didn't want to play ball.

It came to be a source of wonder to me some time later how one is drawn to this type. Essentially violent, powerful men who were outside the circle of normal people. Yet there's no denying it, I was drawn to him and then came to worry whether he was going to be indicted, along with Hoffa, in what turned out to be known as the Chattanooga trial, this time on jury tampering.

That's why when I walked into Nick's Bar one evening I wanted to hear if he was in trouble. Instead, he was acting the big shot. You would have thought Gov. Long had walked in the way everyone was trying to buy him a drink, although actually he did not drink that much. It was a little unusual for Nick's to be this packed on a Thursday, but I guess it was an early warm-up for the weekend.

Who should be at the other end of the bar but Bobbie Jo and Jordan. That was normal for Bobbie Jo, but it was strange to see Jordan sitting on a barstool. There wasn't a lot of work in Cypress Parish so Bobbie Jo and Jordan both worked at the insane asylum. Crazy, good-hearted Bobbie Jo belonged there—I mean the asylum and the barstool. Jordan was from New Orleans and a registered nurse, unlike Bobbie Jo, and better looking. Not coarse. She took her patients to heart, especially the old ones in the geriatrics ward. She and I dated a lot and I knew they could get her down. Some of the patients were clever enough to try to get out. The bloodhounds normally tracked them down, although the local wits said these dogs could only follow the scent if it was down the middle of the rail-road track.

Bobbie Jo was trying to yell over the noise for me, but it was like a canary singing in a windstorm. She kept waving her arm and I skipped the crowd around Jake and went over. Both of my friends were lit up and seemed to be happy.

"Where you been hiding yourself, Cory?"

"Down that dirt road where I live, trying to keep everything fed."

Soon one of Bobbie Jo's running buddies dropped a quarter in the jukebox and got Bobbie Jo off her stool. Something by Jerry Lee Lewis came on which set Bobbie Jo to gyrating and popping her hips back and forth. The men in the bar around Knight refocused. Bobbie Jo's mama had been in Nick's one night when her daughter was dancing and said, "Bobbie Jo in a room full of men is like dragging meat through a dog yard."

After the dance, others started slow dancing and Jake came over.

"Look what the cat drug up," remarked Bobbie Jo. Jake pinched her and she slugged him in the stomach, hurting him a little I could tell, but he wouldn't show it. After a couple of drinks he asked Jordan to dance, which was natural enough, but he had never done it before and I hated to see her body (mine) so close to him. She seemed to enjoy herself, which made it worse, but what the hell. It was a passing thing, and I knew I was just being jealous. What I really wanted to do was get him off in private and ask what was the score about the indictment.

And then something got started that gave me the reds. Knight got to talking about the dogs with several guys at the bar, and one guy, the one who ran the parish road grader, said he had seen wildcat tracks over near a little railroad spur. And Knight allowed that his dogs (his mind you) would as soon run cat as fox, especially if they were put right on the tracks. The dogs were in a pen at my place and I was the one who fed 'em. The next thing I know, half the bar has been invited on a hunt that very night. Which no doubt gave Nick the red ass too, because all the booze was going to stay on the shelf.

Bobbie Jo thought this was the greatest thing that could have happened, and so did Jordan. Neither one was dressed for the woods, though. For me to have tried to talk our way out of it would have made me look bad, but I hated going. Running the dogs had always been a special thing for me, and something you did only with good friends. A private thing. But Knight was just using the dogs to be a big shot. He was probably trying to get as many friends as he could with all the trouble coming his way.

Well, the caravan took off. Everyone was to go to the railroad tracks, where they went into the woods, and we, Jake and I and the two women, would go get the dogs.

I didn't say much, and I wanted Jake to ask what was the matter so I could tell him what was the matter, but he never did.

Everybody was waiting impatiently when we got there, and after Harold the road grader showed us the old tracks, we dumped every hound out at the same time. There wasn't a bit of moon. The only light was from what people made with their flashlights, which wasn't much. Our hands were blue with cold, and a lot of people weren't dressed warmly enough (it looked just like what it was, a crowd pulled out of a cocktail lounge), so right off there was a shout for a big fire.

Once that got going, I took a big medicine bottle out of my jumper and had a drink of whiskey. I had filled it with grandpa's whiskey (it was nearly all gone now) before I left the house, because bringing beer would have been too much trouble. I offered the bottle to Jordan, who was sitting on the tailgate of the pickup, and she took a big slug. About the time she finished, Jake piped up, "I believe I will." Just started reaching for the bottle, and Jordan smiled and handed it to him. It, with her mouth just on it drinking, and now his. And somehow there was something terribly wrong with this, but if I had tried to explain it to anyone, I would have sounded childish.

When he finished, he offered my whiskey to Harold and his two sons, Pud and Dub. Pud and Dub were big and fat and said no. Which I was grateful for. Harold said to save him some. I really hated this. All the people and the invasion.

The wind had died down, and the pines were still, still. Then Suzy, the old toothless bitch, slit the silence with her crowing mouth just once in a while, trying to work the cold trail up. Old and slow dogs like Suzy were in many ways better than the young, fast ones, because it took more head and less drive to run a cat. Jake had said he once saw one just ahead of the dogs jump spread-eagle in a tall bush and let the whole pack run right under her, never moving. Suzy was the kind of dog that would figure out a back track and most other tricks.

Soon a few other dogs joined in, and before long the dogs had jumped and were running. Wouldn't you know it—a crowd of people, many who had never been hunting with hounds, hearing a good race. Never having to cast dogs for nights on end, sometimes only to hear nothing or else a beginning that just petered out. I guess what I had wanted was for the whole affair to be a failure.

A failure it was not—not for everyone else. The dogs ran as if they had gone mad. With the older dogs to solve any intricate problems and the strong, fast ones to drive the cat, it never had a chance to try many tricks and lose them.

The cat's circles were not near the fire, and so if you wanted to get close, you had to leave and go out into the cold. Knight had already taken several others off in the dark, and so I took Jordan, Bobbie Jo, and Harold down to a slough where I figured the cat was crossing, and we just stood quiet. Jordan and Bobbie Jo sipped whiskey as we waited. Both of them were now loaded.

We could hear the dogs making their swing, still off a good ways, and Harold said maybe we would see it, but it was so dark we couldn't see each other.

By the time we figured what had happened, we could have gone up a tree. The dogs kept coming and kept coming, right at us, and they ran slap through and over us. That dark ball of claw and meanness had passed between all of us and we had never known it.

I had not heard the gut cry of hounds just like that, ever. A deep, savage cry that was as terrible as it was beautiful because it was naked hunger and they had killing on their minds.

We all started running after them, trying to be with them, but they were too fast and could see better in the dark. The briers were cutting our hands and legs, and the women were begging to stop.

Then everything stopped. No more crying hounds' mouths, just a few separate howls. We caught up in a picked-over cotton field. I shined my light and saw one or two of the dogs kind of milling around. Knight and his bunch came in from another side of the field with their light. Somebody let out a scream like he was cut. Then all the yelling. "Over here. Over here!"

The cat was down at the bottom of a row. It was exhausted and was heaving, trying to catch its breath. One dog ventured too close and the cat swiped him across the jaw, sending him yelping away.

Suddenly the cat was gone in the darkness. Just like that. All of us were jumping around and skittish, not knowing where it was. The dogs took off again, but this time with the cat riding a hound's back, a hound named Bob Hayes, after a pawnshop owner. When we found the cat again, more tired than before, Knight got the bright idea to rope the cat and put it in the dog crate.

Jake sent me for the dog trailer and told me to back up close to the cat. He and Harold tied a rope onto the end of a pole and put a noose in the rope. Knight must have seen this in some jungle picture of Frank Buck's. The idea was to loop the cat's head, hold it up to the crate door, and let someone push the cat in with a long limb.

Well, the first go-round Knight got the cat (still altogether out of breath) up in the air, but he had made the rope as long as the stick and the cat swung over to him, brushing up against him, and he went to cussing. He took the loop off, shortened the rope, and the next time we managed to get him inside. Had to push rope and all inside before we could lock the door shut.

Then all the talk started about how famous this was going to be all over the parish. Jake announced that he would park the trailer out in front of his house, and everybody could come by.

Pud and Dub and the rest of their cronies all kept shining their lights at the cat in the trailer. It was on its feet and had managed to tear the soft rope from around its neck. It just stayed far up in the front next to the solid wall. It looked very small, even though it must have weighed thirty pounds. Pud felt compelled to jab at the poor devil with a limb. When the now-revived cat smashed that frail limb to pieces and Pud knocked Bobbie Jo into a brier patch trying to get away, I felt better all around, and I don't know which was worse on Pud, the thorns on the brier bushes or Bobbie Jo pounding him, trying to get up.

We left the fire burning in the barren cotton field and broke up. Everyone went his own way and Jake hooked to the trailer with the trophy. I took Jordan with me down the winding road to my house, and as she dozed off I kept thinking, "This was the first time we had really caught what it was we ran after in the dark. Isn't it funny how still everything gets?"

In the yard as I helped Jordan out her side, she threw up on the grass. Women look different throwing up than men, it seemed to me.

She cried, "Oh, Cory, help me, help me."

And all I could think was, woman, I can't help myself.

Idaho Trout

Dean helped Mike, the younger man, push the drift boat off the trailer and into the Snake River. After they loaded their rods and lunches, Dean parked the truck while Mike pulled the boat over to a protected eddy. This part of the Snake below the Palisades Dam was very swift and today there was lots of water.

When Dean returned Mike already had the oars in position.

"Ready?"

"Shove off and rig up."

Dean eased the boat away from the rocks and sat down in the front seat. He put together his fly rod, and after he fastened his reel to the butt, he ran his leader and line through the guides.

"Here, try this," Mike said, handing him the fly.

"What is it?"

"It's a golden imitation of a stone fly."

Dean turned the fly over in his hand. "It's big." The body was made of yellow foam, with a large wing made of white foam. Wound about the body were several strands of gold tinsel and then some brown and white hair.

"In this river you can use really big flies." Although just in his early twenties Mike spoke with the authority gained from three years of guiding on the Snake. Nice life, thought Dean.

As Mike began to row, the green current tried to sweep them rapidly downstream. "It'll be kinda fast the first mile or two, but it'll slow down."

The boat moved slowly downstream, because Mike was rowing hard upstream. This was to give the fisherman in the front of the boat time to cast several times in the best-looking places. Although Dean had fished many places, this was his first time in a drift boat, and he realized how much work this was for Mike. Dean had met Mike far from Idaho. They both lived in Missouri and Dean had seen a print of flying ducks on the Missouri River. He recognized the scene from the high limestone cliffs and asked the owner of the print where he could buy one. When he met the painter, Dean discovered that they shared a passion for hunting and fishing. Since he was a young artist starting out, Mike had to make his living guiding. When the older man mentioned that one of the books he had written was about the Arkansas River, the younger one had invited him up to fish the Snake. "Come see one of my rivers," he grinned.

Right after they swept around a bend and the dam was out of sight, he rowed Dean within casting range. As they drifted and the older man cast, Mike would occasionally say, "That's a good spot over there, under that overhang" or "Let it drift around that rock." Almost as soon as he started casting, he got a strike, but he was too quick setting the hook. As he compensated for this, he was too slow on some others. Even missing many fish, he had the fastest one hour of trout fishing he had ever had. Fifty strikes in an hour. He finally got the right rhythm for setting the hook, even for the lazier cutthroats. He landed and released perhaps twelve to fifteen trout, and just as good, he had hooked all three species on the Snake: browns, rainbows, and cutthroat.

Dean insisted on rowing some once the river slowed down in order for Mike to fish and they swapped places. He had rowed before of course, but not in a drift boat, and not persistently upstream. True, it would have become second nature after hours or days of it, but in such a short time, his rowing was awkward and Mike was frequently too far from the bank for good casting. Trying to row thinking too much about it didn't work. The rowing and the man had to become like one, just like casting.

The two men pulled up on a pebbly sandbar where the river divided with wide areas of riffles. Mike had seen something Dean had missed. Trout were turning over, tailing a little, as they searched for food among the small rocks. They changed to mayflies and added dropper nymphs, eased into the cold water, and almost immediately began catching trout. The trout were in a frenzy of feeding and as soon as one man released his catch, the other's reel began to sing.

Dark clouds, at first small, moved swiftly across the Caribou Range as they waded and fished, but soon a huge bolt of lightning struck a mountaintop in the distance.

"Now I understand how fishermen get hit by lightning," laughed Dean. "It's when the fish are biting like crazy."

Mike kept looking back toward the nearest mountains and when another huge bolt struck and the wind picked up, he moved toward the boat. "Looks like we're going to get wet." They piled into the boat and he began rowing, not against the current now, but hoping to make it to the takeout.

It was not to be and he crossed over beneath a high cliff where the wind could not drive the rain so hard against them. They slipped into their slickers and hunkered down. Even with the slickers they still were soaked. Both tried to take quick bites of their turkey sandwiches then stick them under the slickers, but it was mostly a joke. Dean gave Mike his gingerbread muffin and tried to eat his potato chips before they got wet.

Although he had become cold (it had been so hot in July he had not thought to bring anything warm), he was contented feeling the rain pelt his slicker. He thought back over the morning's action. The Snake was famous for its trout, but he knew that his success had been because of Mike's skill and experience. He respected any skill anyone had, any mastery, any craft, whether it be cabinet maker or chef, athlete or mechanic. Just so he was intensely interested in something.

As the rain became mostly a drizzle, they left for the takeout they had paid a man to ferry their truck and trailer to. With the boat loaded they followed the Snake several miles along the road, then turned again and climbed to the pass. Along the rock road, Dean saw lots of paint-brushes and coneflowers. He kept looking until he saw some columbine. All of these reminded him of the time he followed the Arkansas that began high in the Rockies. He spent a lot of time learning about the plants, especially those that could survive above treeline.

He had grown up around river deltas and swamps full of alligators that could pull you beneath the surface of a bayou until you drowned, and also full of great cypresses with Spanish moss hanging from them like the hair of a weeping woman, and blue hyacinths stretching for-ever on the water. In the mountains it seemed a miracle that some of these colors, like great brushstrokes of paint, could make their way through such small cracks and crevices where there was almost no soil.

When they returned to Driggs, he said, "You're going to let me take you to supper later on, aren't you?" He knew Mike didn't go out to eat much, but saved what money he could from guiding so he could paint in the winter.

Back at his rented cabin, Dean showered, put on some shorts, and made himself a big vodka martini. With his feet propped up on the porch rail, he looked out over the Teton River valley and thought about the trout that he had landed, but just as happily of all the trout that had struck his fly and gotten away, some because of their skill, some because of his lack of it. He began to feel the warm glow of the vodka and made himself another drink. When he came back to the porch, the people who had rented the cabin next to his thought the proper thing to do in this pretty river valley was to turn on the radio and also to turn it up very loud. He guessed that was what made him edgy and started the day downhill by the time Mike came to pick him up. The third drink had made him even less receptive to the music.

Mike picked him up in his beat-up truck and took him to one of his favorite hangouts in the next little town for spareribs. They sat outside and ordered draft beers while a local picked slowly on a banjo. It was tourist season.

Before the ribs came, they had another draft each and Mike steered the conversation to painting. He asked many questions about how to promote his work and business questions about "making it." Since

Dean had published books, Mike wanted to know how to publish books of paintings. Gradually the older man became annoyed with the conversation. No doubt his lack of patience had started with the blaring, adolescent music back at the cabin, and now, with the mountains in the background, talk of "making it" didn't fit.

"You ever think about just sticking with guiding? It's a healthy life and not full of so much bullshit." The remark had been unexpected; Dean's mood had turned.

"How you mean?"

"Kid, you'll have to wade up to your ass in alligators in the art world. It's just as twisted as the literary world. If you're lucky, a gallery will handle your stuff for a third. That's supposed to be the cut. But the alligators want bigger cuts than that. Fifty percent. And then they figure they're doing you a favor. As far as they're concerned, they make the artist. Look at the word they use—'packaging.' They're going to 'package' you. You want to be a package?"

Mike didn't say anything for a bit. Just took a long drink of his beer. Then, "It's not all roses guiding. I mean, when you get a jerk for a client, it's not very pleasant."

"That's for a day. And I know, people can ruin the most beautiful landscape in the world. Still, you've been out in the sun, even the rain like today, you've worked your body, a body that was meant to hunt and fish, to row . . . it works up an appetite. Always encourage your appetites. What kind of life is it to stay in a room by yourself all day, whether you're painting or writing? I know a guy who could have played football . . . he had some talent for that, but took up writing. He sat in an eight-by-eleven room for the next forty years smoking, leaving his cell three times a week to teach school. He was stark white, like those blind fish they find in caves in the Ozarks. He even makes fun of people who soak up the sun like we did today. More worried about skin cancer than living." Just then the baby-back spareribs came out. "Speaking of appetites."

They worked on the ribs silently, cutting each rib loose, dripping with spicy barbeque sauce, and gnawing on the bones like any other carnivore. In spite of himself Dean became more dejected. He thought about the book he had turned in to an editor and this bum, this non-writer, volunteered that Dean should not write such pessimistic books, said he could publish this one if Dean could change the ending to something more upbeat. The clerks in publishing who remaindered his books before they had much of a chance, like grocers taking a magazine off the shelf because at least three prudes dead below the neck objected to it. The conglomerate lawyer-accountants who always managed to screw you out of some pittance of royalties.

The waitress came over and took Mike's plate away and looked like she was going to take Dean's until she saw the look in his eyes.

"More beer?" she said instead.

"Sure," his mouth full of sparerib.

"Not for me," said Mike. "I have to take a client out tomorrow."

Mike guided for a prestige lodge, most of whose guests were simply wealthy enough to afford it, but also occasionally the famous or the accomplished came through. While they had stopped to take a piss on the morning float, Mike told a story about an actress who came every year. When the name was mentioned, Dean remembered being absolutely infatuated with her on the screen as a kid. When one of her husbands divorced her, he remembered thinking how stupid the guy must be. She had a stunning beauty, and at Dean's age then, his testosterone level was higher than his bank account. Mike had beached the drift boat while guiding her, and had discreetly walked around some thick bushes, commencing to relieve himself, when low and behold, one of the most famous beauties of the screen world, now in her eighties, was squatting there two bushes over, doing the same. He was the flustered one.

Now at least three sheets to the wind, Dean said, "You think about what I said about guiding. You'll be working out in the kind of world the body was trained for during several hundred thousand years. And who knows, maybe the next movie star you meet will be closer to your age. Get close to her and the two of you can have your own lodge."

"Right," knowing his dinner companion was crocked.

"Stay away from the alligators," he said, puzzling the waitress as he paid the bill, but she didn't care about his eccentricity when he overtipped.

During the night, Dean woke in a sweat, dreaming he was being pulled under the water like he had seen happen once to a crippled duck. Finally came the cool morning.

Mike had given him directions for where he could wade in the Teton River and had even sketched several bends in the river that ran not far from Driggs. He made himself a sandwich to take with him, then filled a big thermal cup of coffee and drove near the little country bridge where he could step into the river. He sat on the tailgate, sipped his coffee, and made his tackle ready. Yesterday the fishing was fast. Today he hoped the pace would be slow. Here the smaller river meandered through private ranches, the cattle grazing up to their bellies in rich grass, putting on weight they would need to make the long Idaho winter.

To the west were the Big Hole mountains and to the east the Grand Tetons, the Big Tits. Nothing like horny French trappers to give you a good name for mountains. On the Arkansas River French trappers had named a big pointed mountain Maumelle, but prudes-in-residence had changed it to Pinnacle Mountain.

He tied on a mayfly imitation with a parachute, a #16 Baetis, courtesy of Mike who said this often worked. He drained the last of the coffee, put his sandwich in his fishing vest, then slipped over the bank into the cold water. It was always a shock, but within minutes, he felt part of the river and did not notice the cold. Soon he was out of sight of the road and only the cows looked up, the skittish younger ones ready to run at the first thing they did not understand.

He made some casts into very shallow riffles over the gravel, but soon came to the first cutbank that Mike had described. Here the water was not only deeper, but there were places for the trout to hide in ambush. Soon he caught several small browns, and then a tiny ten-inch that came skipping over the water, imitating its bigger cousins. As Dean went about removing the hook with his forceps, he examined the little fellow and realized he had caught his first Idaho Brook trout. Even though he had caught big ones in northern Canada, this small fish made the day start out special. He believed they were not that common in this valley.

Slowly he moved around the large bend, all cutbank, and with the slowed action, looked around as he cast. An osprey whistled "yewk, yewk" sharply as it hunted along the river. Dean marveled at him as he kept casting, and, bam, he missed what seemed to be a big fish. Got to be philosophical about this, he joked to himself. You're here in this beautiful valley. He took a bite of his sandwich while he stood in the water, letting his line trail downstream, gazing at the Big Tits to the east. Bam. A trout had hit his trailing fly while he wasn't even casting. You better start concentrating.

He focused on every cast now, continuing around the cutbank, dropping the mayfly ahead of a small rock or a fallen lump of bank, mending his line, then drilling his attention to the fly. He approached where a rail fence met the river and here Mike had said that in the big riffle was a really good place. With expectations high, he moved quietly through the water, waiting to cast until he was just in the right position. Nothing. He cast again. Nothing. In some way he felt he was being punished for not paying attention before, that there was some secret compensation taking place. Better stop thinking like that, like some kind of Indian. Like the Great Spirit is watching you.

He started back fishing the opposite bank. Several clouds of gnats moved in their whirling little nebulae high above the water. As the river narrowed he moved to the middle in order not to frighten the trout waiting under the leaning branches, when a fish jumped right in front of him. He cast upstream a little from the jump and was hooked up. After admiring the yellow outline of the cutthroat's jaw, he released him, suddenly seeing trout rising everywhere, sometimes eight and ten at a time. Almost every time he cast he got a strike or a hookup. Out in the middle was not where the action was supposed to be, but the trout did not know it. He guessed he must be surrounded by a couple hundred trout and he was standing in the middle of the vortex, this rising.

By the time the miracle had run its course, he had landed six more trout, rainbows and browns. After ten or twelve troutless casts, Dean crossed to a gravel bar and sat down against a fallen log. He must have disturbed a killdeer for it was fussing. "Dee, dee, dee." Probably had some eggs right on the gravel in a little hollowed nest. He took out what was left of his sandwich and munched on it, reveling in the day. Now that he had stopped casting, he could take in the ranch land and the mountains that it led up to, could look at the cloud formations that were beginning to build, and listen to the sounds of the moving water.

Doing was sure different from thinking about it. Casting a dry fly with skill, setting the hook at the right moment, swinging your shotgun on fast-moving mallards, making love. Great pleasures of the physical world, connecting with it. What a poverty without these connections. While you're doing it, you forget everything around it—just you and the fish, you and the woman. That's how he missed those first trout, looking off at the Grand Tetons, missing what was closer to him. Well, he had made up for it, he thought.

He remembered the fishing log he kept wrapped in a waterproof packet, took it out and the stub of a pencil with it, and entered the trout he had caught, first the tiny brook, then the cutthroat and the others, the strongest fish being a rainbow. He noted the #16 Baetis fly, the river (he didn't think he would forget that, though), and the time of day. He told himself that he kept the log so that he could become a better fisherman. That was true, of course. He could avoid certain mistakes of the past, using too heavy a leader, too big a fly. Yet the log was more than that. He felt compelled to do it, as if somehow the fish, the river, would be lost, that they would have been for nothing. Like a universe with not one mind in it to give testimony.

He had from time to time had doubts about so much time spent thinking about things, about all the note-taking, about what had happened. He envied the lucky ones he thought mostly just *did* and who simply kept on doing, leaving any record making to others. But writing about a great love is surely a way of doing homage, of making testament.

The osprey was back, wheeling overhead, searching for his own connection to what he needed. This osprey will not be wasted, he insisted, and made a note in the log.

With a shudder he remembered what had happened last night at dinner, what he had said to the young painter who was trying to find his way. How rotten to have let his own bad memories poison the kid's way.

He jumped up and went striding through the shallow water toward his truck, startling the killdeer again. I must catch him when he comes off the river, I must explain.

Belle Slough

Adam struggled his way up through darkness to the light. Clay Calloway, his hunting buddy and host, had opened the door to the hall, allowing the soft light in. Clay didn't have to say anything, just went into the kitchen to start coffee. They had to meet some other hunters an hour before first light. Being awakened at three in the morning was hard enough, and Adam felt grateful that he and Clay were past the age of horseplay, the kind he remembered in Army barracks and at college. That would have made the early hour even harder.

They had gone to bed early. In spite of a couple of bourbons they still turned in at a decent hour. He noticed he was doing that differently now too. Getting older was odd. He mostly did the same things and felt no differently inside, but being fifty subtly changed things. He was not always able to put his finger on the changes, but they were there. One thing he knew certainly, he ached more when he first got up and sometimes at the end of the day.

There were probably more ducks in Louisiana where Adam often hunted, but he had come to Arkansas for the reason many men hunt anyway, the companionship. For several years he had stopped hunting and spent his time taking pictures of wildlife. Taking pictures outdoors led one to do some of the same things hunting required—both took you outside where it was important whether there was rain or snow, clouds or bright sun. One had to get to know the birds and animals better in order to get closer to them for a picture. Adam liked to take pictures. The craft compelled him to pay attention to light. It mattered very much whether a bird was backlit or not, whether the creature was in overhead light that left no shadows, or in the many shades of red and yellow as the earth turned first toward its sun, and later away.

Yet taking pictures was not the same. There was not the sense of completeness one had after a successful hunt. Also, if the weather was dark or rainy, the photographer didn't go out. With hunting, especially with the short seasons allowed by game laws, one had to hunt when it was time. Or not hunt at all. With duck hunting the weather was almost always cold and as often as not included rain.

The truth was, he sometimes hated to get up early, like this morning, and wondered why he did it. It was like a ritual, though, and once it was time for the ritual to begin, it had to begin. Once it was under way, especially after first light, then Adam knew he was right to have come.

He put on thermal long johns, then a thick wool shirt, next two pair of wool socks and his insulated overalls. The overalls were new. He nearly turned into an icicle last year because he had some leaky waders. The overalls were waterproof, and even if there was a small leak, at least his legs would stay warm. He slipped into some loafers and went for his first hot cup of coffee. He mused that hunters fifty thousand years ago probably didn't start their day with hot tea or hot coffee. But who knows? Once the Chinese, or whoever it was, discovered the hot morning beverage, they stayed with a good thing. Cleaned out all the pipes in the head. Adam couldn't figure out what use sinuses ever had. Maybe Stone Age hunters had some use for them; maybe they didn't have sinus trouble either.

Adam and Clay had to whisper because Clay's wife was sleeping and intended to keep sleeping. Clay grinned broadly, acknowledging the absurdity of getting up in the cold at this hour. He was tall with a ruddy, Scottish complexion, and still carried himself like the Army officer he had been for twenty years before he took early retirement.

"Going to be twenty-five degrees this morning," he remarked.

"We got to be pretty smart characters to go stand in a swamp up to our waists. With that kind of brains, I think we better get some government work."

"It'll build character. At least that's what my old first sergeant used to tell the men."

"I've got about all the character I can stand."

They got their shotguns and shell bags, and each stuck a sandwich in his heavy, camouflaged coat. Outside, Clay's Labrador whined and jumped to the top of the fence. "Not today old podnuh," he replied. The water would be too deep, and they were going to have to wade in. The dog, "Beau," nicknamed for General Beauregard, was beside himself when he was not put in the truck.

The night before, the two men loaded what decoys they could stuff into large net bags they would have to carry into the woods with them. Also their waders and coats. Adam was hoping not to be baptized with swamp water this time out. Clay packed his pipe and lit it, and they started on the hour's drive to Belle Slough. Neither man spoke much, and it was then Adam turned his mind to last night's phone call from his wife. She opened quickly with, "I've got some bad news."

"OK. Let's have it." She knew he didn't like to have anything else said right then except the bare, bad news.

"Rutledge died. Of a heart attack. They're going to bring him back home for burial. The funeral's day after tomorrow."

This meant Adam could hunt only one day, then drive for six hours and still make the funeral. The call came after he and Clay relaxed before the fireplace with some bourbon and ice and commenced to remembering past hunts, especially funny parts when they got stuck, or wet, or something worse. Such moments were becoming more and more important to both of them.

Adam was surprised and a little bewildered, but Rutledge's dying hadn't sunk in. He knew it had happened, but it was more like *knowing* something from television. Not a real knowing, but as if he had been *made aware* of something. Now, though, as he and Clay drove silently through the dark morning toward Belle Slough, Adam realized he had thought about Rutledge in his sleep.

Adam was one of the rare ones who had not had anyone close to him die. Even his parents were still living. His wife, on the contrary, had lost most of her family. Having Rutledge die was a strange experience. He and Rutledge had gone to school together, kept in touch. Sometimes his friend was on the other side of the world, but still they exchanged the occasional letter. Rutledge was a writer who made his living in magazine journalism. He had a staccato, hard-hitting style that sold well, especially adapted to writing about war. The violence attracted him, Adam thought, but he would deny that it did. He insisted it was just a way to make a living while he saved money to write his serious stuff. He was thinking about novels, but he was also a poet. He had the good sense to know he couldn't make a living writing poetry. For the last two years he covered one of the interminable Middle East wars, hoping to stick out a long hitch and return with enough loot. Now he was dead.

Belle Slough was a hardwood bottom that stayed mainly dry during the year and then was deliberately flooded just before duck season so the birds would come in to eat the rich acorn crop. It was a popular hunting area and close enough to large towns that hunters could come out. What this meant was, to get away from all the other guns, locals had to wade deeply into the flooded timber. Clay and some others had reconnoitered the good spots before the season started and most of the time could find them in the dark.

A few cars were already at the jumping off point when Adam and Clay drove up. Stepping out of the warm truck was a shock, but the crisp air was invigorating. Two of the men were newcomers and were introduced to the others. Anybody who was invited was vouched for by one of the regulars. One year a guest peppered another hunter with shot as he tried to finish off a wounded duck trying to get away. Somehow that was more than an accident; it was obscene. After the initial confusion and excuses, no one talked for the rest of the hunt. A great embarrassment.

There was not much time for talk this morning as Clay and Adam slipped on their boot liners, then struggled clumsily into the long chest waders. Each helped the other put a big bag of decoys on his back and they were ready to go. Even in the sharp cold, Adam worked up a sweat before they got to the water's edge. Most of his body heat was trapped in the waders and heavy coat.

Single file, they stepped off into the black water. The leader had a small light, and the rest tried to avoid the sunken limbs and stumps or sudden potholes. Last year one of the group fell into the cold water on the way in. His waders filled up and he had to trudge freezing back to the car.

Finally they came to a space ringed with oaks and began to spread the decoys. Groups of drake and hen mallards with a few wood ducks on the outer edges. The wind blew from the west and the floating decoys nearly all faced into it. The ducks would fly in from the east to land, into the wind, so each hunter found a tree he could stand next to from where he could see the incoming birds. Adam loaded his twelve gauge with No. 4s and then leaned against his tree. He broke away the ice ringing the trunk at water level.

Rutledge was still on his mind. They had hunted together once, years back, but the hunt had not been good. Rutledge came dressed for the hunt in a Confederate cavalry hat with a large yellow plume, a great brass CSA buckle on his belt, and smoking a long slender cigar. Some of the other dove hunters looked on amazed. For someone who talked a lot about guns and killing, Rutledge did not shoot well. He made the mistake of drinking before he took to the dove field, and that was just enough to make him miss. Still, when he wrote about it, the hunt turned out beautifully, he had shot well, and he transformed the whole day into a good time.

Adam chided him about the difference between real life and his story, said that there were those who could do and those who could write about it. Rutledge just smiled.

Now Rutledge was gone. His *goneness* surprised Adam, but also he was surprised how the proximity of death, any death, had been kept out of mind for such a long time. He remembered the story in the Bhagavad-Gita, where the god Dharma, in the figure of a crane, asks which of all the world's wonders is the most wonderful, and the answer had been that no man, though he sees others dying all around him, believes he himself will die. Adam extended this even to the ones around him. He remembered having two young dogs, litter mates, that spent their puppy days wrestling and chasing each other until one day a car killed one. For an hour the other dog stayed close by, nudging his brother to begin play again, clearly at a loss. Adam felt like the puppy that had been left.

Just the faintest light showed itself, and he could see most of his fellow hunters outlined against the trees. Slowly the circle of water became a mirror in the increasing light. Taking pictures had forced Adam to remove himself from what was happening in order to plan his shots. It had become a habit, this standing off from things. He imagined photographing this circle of men around the undulating, watery mirror. He would have to be high up for the scene to mean anything to a stranger. Even then, what would it mean unless the viewers had some intimate knowledge of hunters, of their minds? Unless they participated.

Inevitably Adam felt Rutledge's death instructing him. Both men had a wide streak of futurism in them, planning what they were going to do years ahead. Adam felt this was more becoming in undergraduates, but knew it to be an affliction. Planning to be happy. So much of this future never happened.

There was old Rutledge slated for the black hole, where there was no time, no future, no present. Funny about time and space. In space one could reverse direction. He could, and would, wade back through flooded woods to the truck, then to Calloway's, to his small-town law practice and good wife. But time went only one way, and Rutledge had fallen off its arrow. Now the money he saved and the time he saved up for had no meaning.

Unless he hunted, Adam was seldom up at sunrise; the light on the water and against the limbs and trunks of the winter oaks took his breath away. What a beautiful earth! This beauty seemed to be hidden by so many things: filing briefs, searching vendor and vendee records in the courthouse, taking the car to be fixed, going to the dentist, the indoorness of modern life, the general paving of country with highways, shopping malls, parking lots. We have cut ourselves off from the sun and stars. Now we send our proxies to the moon and Mars. Beyond the surfaces of the earth the heavens are conveyed to us on the television screen. A proxy vision.

Just then the leader of the procession through the dark broke the silence with his hailing call for mallards. He had seen some green-heads zipping along above the treetops and was trying to turn them. Immediately Calloway broke in with his beseeching hail. This was one of the best parts of duck hunting, Adam thought. Talking to the animals. To know the language of animals is a magic, a way of passing through an inscrutable barrier, a way to get beyond the surfaces to some deep down thing. Both men began the clucking of feeding ducks, trying to draw the circling birds to them.

Adam lost sight of the ducks because he kept his face down so as not to be seen, showing only the camouflage of his hat. They would shy away if they saw an upturned face. "Here they come," the closest hunter whispered, and from the east they were dropping through the trees, wings flared for landing when the farthest shooter opened up and a single drake dropped to the water while the others beat frantically for height. Adam's heart raced as the others managed to escape. Such an ecstasy! The mallards, the oak, the hunters, all one brilliant convergence of design!

While the successful hunter waded for his duck, the others resumed the vigil by their oaks. Everyone was much more alert now since this first eruption out of the breaking dark. What if life could be like such peaks, Adam thought. Instead, there were great stretches of silence punctuated by swift pleasure . . . and pain. And death. Rutledge's. His very life had been a swift inflorescence, like a solar flare the recent pictures of the sun revealed. Like it, no one knew when the apogee would occur. Like the sudden appearance of the mallards, Rutledge emerged out of the mystery, then returned to it. Each scene leaving one death. Both appearances concentrated time into nodes of beauty before the falling away.

For a moment Belle Slough became the Slough of Despond for Adam, but he jerked himself back to the present. Deep in the woods he heard the rising whistle of a wood duck. Clay picked out his one wood-duck call from his lanyard and whistled back. Again, the

shaman magic of talking to the unseen birds. Adam promised himself again to practice his calling during the off-season. Since he was
not skilled, he deferred to the initiated.

Suddenly their circle of hunters seemed to be a spiraling vortex
for all the wood ducks in Belle Slough. "Two hens at ten o'clock!"
Clay yelled, both he and Adam catching the two hens in the midst
of oak limbs and stunted trees. Again the racing of the heart as the
birds plummeted to earth. Adam waded out and picked up his first
of the day. As he returned to his tree, he realized he had forgotten a
bag to put his kills in. He dropped the hen between himself and the
trunk of the tree, hoping it would float there, but spent the rest of
the hunt keeping his kills from drifting away in the slow, impercep-
tible current.

Almost immediately there was shooting to their right and left,
and the woods were alive with ducks. Even though four or five
hunters fired, still the wood ducks came, as if willingly meeting the
hunters. They were used to feeding on the acorns every morning at
this spot, and they were going to come, hunters or not. Like
humans, Adam thought, they changed their behavior only under the
whip of necessity.

There was a danger now that someone would follow the flight of
a duck through the labyrinth of limbs and finally swing his shotgun
on line with another hunter. Just as it was difficult to follow two rabbits at once, it was difficult to keep one eye on a flying wood duck
and one out for eight other hunters. Now and then someone yelled,
"I'm over here, over here!" to warn the busy shooter.

The daily limit had been changed again this year and some were
still confused about the law. The limit was three ducks, but no more
than two hens. Adam knew his third duck had to be a drake, and
consequently he had to shoot with great control. A pair came speed-
ing through the trees to Clay's left, and he snapped off a shot, watched
his final bird hit the water. His shot marked a lull in the shooting.
The men began to talk quietly, everyone relaxed with the good luck.

"It's a hard job," grinned Clay, "but someone has to do it."

"You're right," Adam agreed. "Laboring over a hot shotgun all day."

Soon there was quiet again. The wind stopped and the pool they stood in was unruffled, now mirroring everything above it. Even the floor of the swamp was visible, leaves and stumps standing out clearly in the bright morning sun. The crowded sounds of early morning frogs and insects, of crows and a hundred perching birds, subsided. Clay twice blew the mournful whistle of the wood duck. Adam concentrated on the woods behind him.

Then the whirring wings of a drake whipped in from the right, and with a smooth, unthinking movement, Adam pointed. Just then the drake passed through a bright shaft of light, and all the reds, blacks, and greens seemed to catch fire, to show forth some unleashed divinity in a forest epiphany. In a great coalescence, the bird and Adam became one. And he tumbled from the air.

"That winds it up," Clay said as Adam waded through the oaks to retrieve the fallen duck.

He picked up the bird carefully, examining the almost carved lines of color. "Well, old fellow, you make the limit," said Adam.

Clay loaned him a piece of cord to tie his ducks together. He then tied the cord to his belt and the three ducks floated behind as he helped to pick up the decoys and stuff them into the net bags. Everyone was talking happily as the men waded for the decoys. Numerous hunts during the last several years had passed with no shooting at all. Fewer ducks were coming from the north because the thousands of potholes and small pieces of wetlands had been plowed under.

Adam was beginning to feel like a dinosaur. The world had changed so fast that he and his ways were going to be extinct soon. He had a feeling of helplessness mixed with anger. Was the whole world going to be turned into the slums of New York and Calcutta? Sometimes Adam felt many humans must have a tremendous resentment against nature, like hating your mother and father, intent on blotting out the memory of the source. That somehow their birth hadn't been tidy, tidy like their city apartments. A fastidious urban Puritanism. Like life was only an idea.

Finally all the decoys were packed. Soon the men were wading single file back through trackless water. The walking, or trudging, was not as difficult as it had been in the dark, but still there was the sudden hole to watch for. Adam was at the end of the procession, sometimes falling behind as he went back in time, remembering Rutledge, flying ducks, and many things that had been and were no more.

Long before there were large cities, Anaximander wrote that it was necessary for things to perish into that from which they were born, for they paid one another penalty for their injustice according to the ordinance of Time. This had puzzled Adam when he first read it. Now he thought the old Milesian was expressing the way, the *tao*, that darkness becomes light, and then the return to darkness, the ascendancy of birth and growth and the falling away. In the flux of things, there was that which gathered itself into being, now a flower, now a duck, a poet. This gathering reached its limit, then fell away into the limit of death. Perhaps the way small waves make their procession and flash beautiful with the light, then descend to the formless water of the fecund swamp.

The attempts to deny these limits, which Adam found rampant nowadays, filled him with dread and even disgust. The limit on ducks was a meager one, but a necessity. Clay and he both knew hunters who killed whatever flew in front of them, missing a great point. They were no different in kind from the big-time urban marauders and poachers. Devil take the hindmost.

Ritual, even etiquette, seemed to have disappeared in Adam's lifetime. What was left was naked appetite, unbound to any necessity. Adam had the eerie realization that he was part of a dying civilization, and, with the speed of current events, the end would not be long in coming. Well, he must do what he could, but he felt pessimistic for his children, just beginning their adult lives.

At last the men emerged from the water and shadowy swamp After their legs had pushed against water for so long, they suddenly felt the change of bounding into a lighter medium. Like the speeded-up transition of a sea creature adapting to land.

Back on the road, they were happy to divest themselves of their load of decoys, their game and guns. Then to emerge from their chrysalis of waders and heavy coats. Back to normal. They stood around briefly retelling some of their shots, laughing at their misses, then shook hands all around.

Back home, after giving Beau a pat on the head, they took their six ducks to the back yard. Clay had made a bench out of some thick planks and left it under a big tree. He cleaned his fish there in the summer, his game in the winter.

"Let's breast most of them. Maybe just keep the mallard whole," Clay said. He cut an incision down the middle of the breast just under the skin line. Adam held the skin apart while Clay cut gently down the breast bone, then under the breast. From each duck there were two thick red pieces. The feathers and carcasses were in a bag nearby.

"Something to remember the hunt by," grinned Adam, taking one of the prettiest feathers from a male wood duck. He stuck it in his hat.

Soon there was a rosy pile of meat on the bench top. Plucking the mallard was a longer task, but when they finished, the bird lay intact. Three of the shot pellets had left dark marks across the breast, like stigmata. Both men washed their hands and rinsed the pieces of meat.

"Let's get these breasts in some oil and a little wine. I normally like to soak them for twenty-four hours, but since you'll be pulling out in the morning, we'll do the best we can."

Right, thought Adam. Got to bury Rutledge tomorrow. Wonder where he's lying right now? Closed up in a box in an unfamiliar room.

Carol, Clay's wife, had left a note that she was shopping. After Clay mixed the marinade for the breasts, he said, "I don't know about you, but I could stand a shower and a little snooze."

"Sounds good," agreed Adam. Later, on his bed, he reflected how abruptly death had taken his friend, how unnatural it seemed. There's always that problem, trying to explain suffering and death. He doubted he would ever get it right. What to do in the meantime? Whatever the reason, this was the only world he and Rutledge had: imperfect, unpredictable. But there would be no journey, nothing to do, if all of it was perfect and predictable. Guess you have to do with life what Rutledge did with his story of the good hunt where he shot well. Transform it. Take the gold from the ore. And show your panache. Why not? He smiled as he remembered his friend firing away at the incoming doves, the feathers in his cavalry hat waving audaciously in the breeze. Adam knew he better start paying attention. With this he fell into sleep.

He was awakened by the delicious smell of baking bread. After dashing some cold water in his face, he found Clay in the kitchen with Carol. "The old girl decided to bake in your honor," smiled Clay.

"I figured the mighty hunters would be starving," she said. Clay began retrieving the breasts from the marinade.

"Let me help," Adam said. He felt a need to be a part of the cooking. Not just a spectator. He wound each half breast in strips of bacon. The bacon fat, he knew, would help baste the lean meat of the breast. The breasts were thick muscle from the rapidly moving wings, dark red because of the need for large amounts of blood.

Soon the breasts were over the coals in the smoker. "They don't take very long," said Clay. "A fellow cooked them like this for the Ducks Unlimited supper last year. He stole the show."

The sun was setting by the time the smoking was finished. As if in a final, triumphant gesture, the sun's rays struck the underside of a line of clouds, bathing the world in its rosy light. At the table the three of them raised their glasses of burgundy in toast. "Here's to next year's hunt," offered Clay.

"Here's to right now," rejoined Adam. With each morsel of the dark meat, he thought how beautiful the duck's flight had been and how beautiful the duck was now. How important it was to eat when one was eating.

Hanging Out, Hanging On

Flying from Houston to San Jose, Dean still carried the heavy load of his divorce with him, like an osprey entangled with a heavy fish it cannot drop. The voices were almost all American and the tasteless food was as bad as the frozen dinners he had been eating since his wife left. Once on the ground, he was diverted by trying to remember his school Spanish enough to get to the hotel and by cocktail hour he was feeling the relief that one has escaping from the place where people know your name and have expectations of you. One of his law partners had regaled him with big fish stories in Costa Rica and so he left, traveling light and enjoying the feeling of having left behind all his keys.

Early the next morning he boarded a small twin-engine plane for the Pacific coast and the little town of Golfito. They winged their way past the Central Valley and soon were over the mountains that finally tilted into the Pacific. Dean was already feeling the relief of escape. He just wanted to hang out, to be the loafer he never was.

The plane came to the coast and turned south, flying low enough that he could see the rocky inlets and the surf. After a quick descent to a very short airstrip, he was soon carrying his luggage toward some vans and trucks. There was no terminal. He looked around for something with his lodge's name on it and was pleasantly surprised to hear a sultry-looking brunette calling his name. Life is looking up, he thought.

She was all smiles and possessed an easy-going Latin affability. Her name was Consuela and she looked to be in her mid-twenties. Every move she made seemed to say, "I have been waiting for you." Golfito was an old banana town that had been built by United Fruit many years ago, she explained, and as they drove she pointed out the houses where the management had lived. Laid-back architecture with lots of palm trees.

"The boat to the lodge is waiting down at the marina," she remarked casually.

"How long a trip?"

"Just twenty or thirty minutes, depending on the tides."

Womanless for some time, Dean was busy building a tropical fantasy that included Consuela. She smiled at everything he said.

They pulled up near a dock lined with deep-sea fishing boats. Dean got out and put his luggage on the ground just as a short, muscular fellow in shorts came up, saying hello to Consuela, and introducing himself as "Buck, your captain." He picked up the luggage and headed to the boat.

"I hope you enjoy your stay," said Consuela as she headed back to the van.

"Aren't you coming to the lodge?"

"Oh, no, I just pick up the guests."

"Too bad."

She smiled as if he had missed something and drove off.

They cast off and moved down the coast in the small bay or "little gulf," and Dean stood next to Buck under the small sun top in order to hear what was said above the engine noise. In a short time Dean learned that Buck had had a small business in Corpus Christi, Texas, quit it because the taxes and employee benefits were too high, and moved down here. He said he had fished a lot out of Corpus, but also along the eastern Mexican coast with his father, who was a veterinarian. Surfed a lot, too.

The lodge faced the ocean, but they entered a river behind the little peninsula and tied up at the private dock of the lodge. After tidying up the boat, Buck dropped Dean off at his cabin. "I'll check in with you later this evening at the bar. I've got some business I've got to deal with."

"What time do we shove off in the morning?"

"Entirely up to you. Most of the time fellows like to leave around seven. Talk to you later."

Dean slipped into some shorts and a fresh shirt and took in his surroundings. The cabins formed a square around a swimming pool, and from his porch he could hear the surf. Not bad. He unpacked his things, then sat on the porch with his legs propped up and listened to a gentle rain on the tin roof. Around cocktail hour he walked across the courtyard and entered the lodge bar and dining room. Two small women were lying on their backs on a pool table and watching a soap opera on the TV high up on the wall.

The older one sat up after he came in.

"Are you ready for something to eat?" She looked to be thirty-five or forty, a trim figure and petite features.

"Actually I was looking for a drink,"

"Sure. Anything you want," she said as she walked behind the bar.

"How about a vodka martini?"

"We have some vodka. What else goes in a martini?"

"Vermouth."

She looked through twenty or thirty bottles and shook her head. "I don't see any."

"How about just vodka on ice." As she poured, he asked, "Where is everybody, still fishing?"

"You're the only guest. It's the rainy season. Sometime we have a few parties during the rainy season, but most of the people come while it's winter in the States."

The younger woman, somewhat heavier, was still lying on her back on the pool table watching what turned out to be a Brazilian soap opera. Although the older woman stayed behind the bar, her eyes were still riveted to the TV.

Off to one side of the bar-dining room was an office cut off from the noise by glass, but from which the staff could keep track of things. In a few minutes a slender, very tan man came in, went briefly into the office, and put some papers on one of the desks. Soon he came back, offering his hand saying, "You must be Dean. I'm Franz. Sorry I wasn't here to greet you, but I see Theresa has already fixed you up." He poured himself a short drink and leaned on a stool that was behind the bar.

"You're the owner?" Dean asked. His friend stateside had mentioned another name.

"Oh, no. That's Fred. He's got business in Golfito." At that, Theresa looked over stonily from the soap opera.

"No, I just handle a few things in the office."

"Your accent says German."

He smiled ever so slightly. "Yes. Nuremburg."

"How in the world did you get way over here?"

"A long story. But the short version is that I've done a lot of ocean sailing. I sailed to the States and then drifted down here."

"You have a boat here?"

"Not anymore."

As they continued to drink, out of curiosity Dean asked more about Franz's background, and the answers became often oblique, vague. When asked if he was going back to the States, he replied he didn't think so. Somehow there was the hint that Franz had compelling reasons for not reentering the States. He apparently was "on the beach" for a time.

It wasn't long before Dean volunteered his own personal situation and made the crack that it was apparently going to cost him a lot of money for his wife to find herself in California.

"As Nietzsche remarked, 'In revenge and in love woman is more barbarous than man.'"

Finally the steamy Brazilian soap opera was over and both women swung themselves off the pool table.

Theresa returned and asked when he would like to eat.

"How about in an hour?"

"Will grilled fish be ok?"

"Take it," remarked Franz. "It's excellent. Theresa is a fine cook." She looked over appreciatively.

"Then grilled fish."

Franz excused himself and Dean walked out to the beach where the surf was pounding away.

The next morning Dean met Buck at the boat and they left the sheltered waters and traveled a couple of miles still inside the bay. Buck looked for signs of baitfish on the surface and soon they raced over and cut the motor. Two small rods had been rigged with shiny hooks placed a few inches apart for several feet. Each man hurled his set of hooks in the swarm of baitfish, sometimes retrieving his line with nearly every hook filled. Soon the livewell was full of thrashing bait six to eight inches long.

They moved out of the chop of the bay rounding an arm of land with a small mountain, then on to the deeper water offshore. There were five- to seven-foot seas, but the open, twenty-five foot boat took the water well and in another thirty minutes they were rigging up. In rod holders from the transom Buck let out line with big eight-inch lures, one line some twenty-five feet farther out than the other. From the outriggers he used the live bait and these extended much farther back than the lures.

"You have to try everything," Buck remarked, "but chances are they're going to hit that line," pointing at one of the two lines with the lures.

"Why is that?"

"I don't know. It might be some way the hooks hang, or the way the lure moves in the water . . . just a lucky lure. It's not the color. I've used the identical color but it never brings in the fish that one does."

While they trolled, Dean breathed lungs full of fresh, clean air, so different from the city, and except for the twin engines, the only sounds were the breaking water and the seagulls and terns. He saw no other boats, only the background of the green mountains high above the shore. The knots in his stomach were beginning to ease.

After a time of silent trolling, he asked questions about tackle and about fishing techniques. Talk got back to fishing in Corpus Christi, how they fished there, and then the talk slipped right off the deep end. Maybe it had started with some talk about women.

"My dad is doing time in Texas for rape."

"No shit."

"Yeah. He had this young Mexican housekeeper. She kept asking for raises, more raises, and finally my dad told her no. She went to the police and claimed he raped her."

"Just her word against his?"

"She was underage and the judge said he ought to have known better."

"Damn." Not knowing what else to say, he said nothing. Gee, he thought, paradise doesn't last long.

They kept on looking and trolling and then a reel began to whine. "Grab the rod, grab the rod!" Buck yelled.

Dean worked the rod out of the holder and drew it back to set the hook, and the beautiful silver sailfish leaped, trying to throw the pain out of its mouth. He pumped the short, stiff rod, kept reeling, and again the dark blue and silver acrobat threw itself into the air.

Guessing that he might have a prolonged fight on his hands, he looked around for the first time for something resembling a fighting chair, but there was only a plastic chair on the stern which had seen better days. Still, he used it, thinking he might be here for some time.

It was with some surprise that in a short time he brought the fish to the boat. First Buck grabbed the long bill and brought it up over the side, then said, "Here, grab her, grab her, while I get the camera." Dean gripped the bill close to the head while one great eye of the fish stared at him and he concentrated on smiling for Buck's Polaroid photo. Laying the camera on the boat's console, Buck worked the lure out of her mouth and Dean released her.

"We lucked out early. Congratulations," extending his hand to Dean.

"Hope the picture comes out." Sure enough, as the outer film of the photo was peeled back, there she was, her sail unfurled, and the great eye staring.

"Lots of guys come down here and fish for four or five days and never have that kind of luck."

"It was on your lucky lure."

"Yeah. Even the lucky lure doesn't always bring 'em in."

"She seemed easier to bring in than I expected. She weighed almost as much as a tarpon I caught. Are they always that easy?"

"A sailfish is a pussy. Wait'll you hook a marlin."

They continued to troll for a couple more hours without a hook-up but Dean was elated with his first sailfish, how beautiful she was, and how beautiful the day was. He was taken out of himself, felt full of health and promise.

Back at the dock, Buck stayed to put the boat in order and wash it down. As Dean left for his cabin, Buck said he would catch up with him after dinner. He showered and found a cold beer in the small refrigerator in his room. Back on his front porch, he was a contented man, the surf pounding, the palm trees swaying in the slight breeze. Soon he walked past the swimming pool to the lodge bar and was greeted by Theresa who was watching TV, but this time in an upright position.

"Vodka on ice?"

"Right." He belted down his first drink.

"How was the fishing?"

"Caught a nice sailfish. I forgot the picture in my room."

"Lucky hombre." She poured him another.

They chatted some and Dean happened to remember the girl who had picked him up at the airstrip. "The girl who picked me up and brought me to the boat . . . she never works at the lodge, only in Golfito."

Theresa's face contorted in anger. "That bitch. She's nothing but a cheap whore."

Dean knew instantly he had made a mistake, but he didn't know just what kind. He mumbled, "Sorry. It's not important."

She was just warming to the subject. "Filthy slut," and broke into rapid Spanish that Dean could not follow. Finally she began to cry.

Franz, who had been working in the office, came out. "I'll take care of the bar if you want, Theresa."

She went through the kitchen door.

"I think I just messed up."

"What happened?"

"I was talking about my sailfish, then I asked about this other woman who works for the lodge in Golfito."

"Ah," he smiled. "Sorry you had to be troubled by the family quarrel. You see, that's Fred's mistress in Golfito,"

"I still don't quite get it. Is Theresa his mistress, too?"

Franz looked puzzled. "Theresa? No, Theresa is Fred's wife."

"I've stepped into a big pile of it, I think." Buck had not introduced him to anyone. He thought the two women on the pool table were cooks and waitresses. And where was the mysterious Fred? "Who's the other woman in the kitchen?"

"That is Theresa's daughter. Fred is her father. I'm sorry as a guest you had to hear about this," he said in a courtly way.

Soon Theresa came back out to the bar and Franz excused himself. Her eyes still showed her crying.

"What would you like to eat tonight?" she asked bravely. They agreed on shrimp and Dean continued to nurse his drink, looking out to sea. As he drank the sadness of his own broken marriage mingled with his discomfort at Theresa's unhappiness,

Shortly she came back in with his dinner and asked if he wanted to move to a table.

"No, the bar will be fine."

She talked as he ate his food. Same subject as before. "My husband just thinks he can tell me to leave. Well, there are new laws in Costa Rica now."

Dean continued to eat his shrimp.

"That girl in Golfito abandoned her own children. What do you think of that?"

Dean assumed it was a rhetorical question, She began to tear up again.

"I know it must be painful."

"I went to a priest and you know what he told me? That I should find me another man,"

"No kidding?"

"Fred and I built this whole place together. It was just a little café when we started and I did all the cooking. Now he thinks he can just tell me to leave. Well, it's not the old Costa Rica anymore."

"Sounds like you need a good lawyer."

"I went to visit my cousin in San José and she took me to her church. Evangelical. My cousin told me to tell the congregation what was on my heart and I did. Afterwards, they all came up and hugged me. If I go back there even now, they hug me and hold me." She reached under the bar and took out a Bible. "Here, I hold on to this." She weeped some more as she laid the bilingual Bible on the bar. It was one of those the Gideons leave everywhere in motel and hotel rooms or men hand out on street corners. "Do you want more to eat?"

"No, no, I'm fine. I think I'm going to go to bed early. If you're not used to so much sun and wind, you tire quickly."

It was true that he was tired. It was also true that he wanted to escape to his room. What happened to just hanging out? The palm trees were there, the surf was pounding, and even a little rain fell on the tin roof. The scenery was perfect, but none of the actors knew the right lines.

At breakfast early the next morning, he met Fred. Apparently he just came in to check the books. When he walked out of the office, he came over to Dean's table and "welcomed him aboard." A day late. He was a big fellow, not handsome in any way, gone in the paunch, and his eyes seemed to reflect a great banality. Then he disappeared. Dean could hear a boat crank up and he listened as it apparently headed back to Golfito.

Shortly afterward he met Buck at the dock and soon they were catching bait. To Dean the chop in the bay seemed greater than the day before and when they passed the arm of the bay, the seas were clearly bigger than the day before. The outriggers went out, two lines long, two short, one with Buck's lucky lure.

They trolled and they trolled. First for an hour not far from the coast line and in the area where they had hooked the sailfish. After no luck, they moved farther and farther offshore. Nothing. They kept changing areas. There was a lot of time to talk. Dean brought up the trouble with Theresa.

"You know, you didn't introduce me when I arrived and I didn't even know Theresa was Fred's wife, I didn't know who Fred was because he didn't show up until this morning."

"Sorry. Everything seems to be going to hell around here. The reason I didn't hang around that first day was my old lady was leaving me and we had a few things left we had to yell at each other about. That was the business I had to take care of." He smiled. Buck did not smile often and when he did he seemed to be out of practice.

Good grief, thought Dean, is the whole world out of joint?

After another hour Buck spotted a weed line and they began to follow it. On and on. In the distance they could see a furious little squall pouring rain down, surrounded by otherwise calm skies.

"We need to keep a good eye out," Buck reminded them both,

Suddenly, while Buck was checking some tackle Dean saw what seemed to be a long dorsal fin, and he yelled out. It disappeared before Buck could see it, but he swung the boat back around slowly.

"Probably the tail if it's a marlin."

Dean suspected Buck might not have confidence in his sighting, but they returned.

Then it happened and it happened fast. A huge marlin went pounding across the water far off the stern. He ran to pull the rod out of the holder and reared back to set the hook several times. Still the dark blue giant continued to try to throw the pain from his mouth. Suddenly Dean began to know the difference between a sailfish and a marlin. No more leaps. Just pumping the rod and reeling.

After about forty-five minutes, she was finally brought close. Seeing the boat, she ripped off yards and yards of line, and went deep. All the work to do over again. Another half-hour and this time Buck caught the leader while Dean continued to hold the rod, but it was no go. Down again. Dean's mouth was like parchment and he kept asking Buck for water. Pump and reel, pump and reel. Dean was soaked from sweat and finally he threw up the water and what was left of his breakfast.

Buck explained that by international rules, holding the leader is considered a catch, but Dean had wanted somehow to get a picture. He could not let go of the rod for the camera for fear the fish would rip off again and take the rod with her. By the end of the second hour he brought the huge fish alongside and once again Buck grabbed the leader. But the fish was not whipped. Buck grabbed the bill and the marlin jerked the man's whole upper body around.

"I'm cutting her loose before somebody gets hurt." He let her go briefly and grabbed his pliers. Dean realized he was going to try and save his lure instead of cutting the line. Once again he grabbed the bill and tried to work the lure out, but in the thrashing about he cut the line, released the fish which sank out of sight. Buck barked out a string of curses. He had lost his lucky lure.

"Sorry about the lure."

"Sooner or later you lose everything. Bound to happen."

Both of them wound in the lines and folded the outriggers back.

"That mother had to be four hundred fifty pounds if she was an ounce. She was a handful, huh?"

"You said it."

"You must be on a roll."

"Maybe so."

When they got back to the dock Buck said, "You know, you're supposed to throw the guy in the water when he catches his first marlin."

"Tell you what. I'll throw myself in the pool when I get out of these clothes."

"At's a deal. I'll drop over later so we can celebrate your marlin."

At the cabin he turned up the coldest beer he could find and downed it in one pour. With another one in hand he went to the pool and fell into the cold water. Now self-baptized he sat in the breeze stripped of any strength from the tussle with the fish. He was left with a sense of well-being, and all because of a fish and the sun and water. He thought, can it be as simple as this?

Changing into shorts, he brought his sailfish picture with him to the bar.

"Hey, Theresa, look!" and, after she looked, "Caught a marlin today, but no picture," She give him a big hug. He put the photo back in his shirt pocket and had two funny tropical drinks that Theresa insisted were just great, and then slipped back into vodka after he ate some bar food Theresa called tapas.

While she was in the kitchen, he thumbed through her Bible left on the bar and came to a worn page in "Mateo" 5:13: *"Vosotros sois la sal de la tierra; pero si la sal se desvaneciere, ¿con que sera salada? No sirve mas para nada, sino para ser echada fuera y hollada porlos hombres."* First he thought of Theresa—she had lost her savor for Fred and had been cast out. Then he turned it upon himself—how had he lost his savor for his wife? Was he good for nothing but to be cast out and trodden under foot? Better quit thinking like that.

Franz and Buck came in together and he announced that since it was his last day, all drinks were on him. They kept up with him for the rest of the evening.

At dark they walked down the water-soaked sand of the only road in town. In the pitch black, huge dogs rushed up to the fences, but Buck kept saying, "No *importante*. All bluff."

"I'm surprised this place has a bar," Dean joked.

"What? We have two! We just have to see where everybody is tonight."

The village drinkers had settled at the first one they came to. Nearly all of them were expats. He heard one woman speaking French with a fellow from Canada. Quietly Buck identified the characters he knew. A couple of widowers spent some time here, one or two were evading taxes or alimony, and as Buck's voice fell to a whisper, he remarked that one or two couldn't return to their home countries under any circumstances. Of the locals, one was quite drunk, his coarse hair standing out wildly, like he had seen a demon once and never gotten over it.

Buck left his seat and began playing a game Dean had never seen before. On a post in the middle of the room a nail had been driven in, and a ring attached to a long string was on the nail. The object of the game was to stand behind a line and swing the ring so that it landed on the nail. Very high tech sport. Buck ringed the nail three out of four times. He motioned to Dean. "Here, want to try it?"

Dean tried it ten times and missed ten times. Franz wasn't having any of it. He had switched to brandy. The wild-haired local got off his bar stool and decided he could do it. As they watched the local fail at the game, Buck started complaining about his ex-wife. She had apparently taken everything in the house and loaded it on to a boat while he was out with a client. Showing his liquor by now, his arm around Dean's shoulder, he said, "But that's what it's all about, right? Catch and release. Catch and release fish, catch and release women."

The local kept missing and Franz became more serious with every drink. Dean took his sailfish picture out and showed Franz.

"Yes," he said thoughtfully, *"Ichthus,"* and wrote the word in Greek with spilled beer on the bar. "Something to hold on to, that fish," he ended mysteriously. "Good for later memories."

"You studied Greek?"

"Yes, before I was kicked out of seminary."

The drunk kept missing the nail with the ring.

While Buck flirted with a woman to his right, Franz looked about the bar and said, "Most of these ladies and gentlemen are 'on the beach.' As our friend Nietzsche wrote once in a letter, 'Broken on the wheel of their own feelings.'"

"I think I've been under the wheel myself for the last several months."

"Self-pity and resentment are unhealthy." The bartender poured him another brandy. "All experiences are useful. Even divorce. Now you can become a new man. You can overcome yourself." He raised his glass to Dean. "To the new man, although the old man has been generously buying the drinks."

By now the local had missed the nail at least a hundred times. He stumbled angrily back to his stool. Buck turned and whispered to Dean, "I'm going to mess with the guy's head a little." As Buck picked up the ring, the local stared sullenly at him. One swing of the ring and it settled on the nail.

"Franz, good sir, I think it's time to get out of here," said Dean. "I've got to catch a plane in the morning."

The next morning he gave Theresa another big hug after breakfast and said his goodbyes to Franz. "Give me a call if you get stateside."

He laughed. "Don't think I'll make it back there. Life on the beach is not so bad even though it doesn't fit the States' idea of a good worker."

On the boat trip back to Golfito with Buck, he tried to take special note of the mountains, the surf, the lodge from the oceanside seen through the palms. At dockside in town, he gave Buck a lavish tip, making him happy. The lodge van this time had Fred and Consuela in it. They were taking a trip to San José, too.

As the little plane bounced its way off the airstrip a woman jogged nonchalantly along the concrete doing her morning run. Fred and Consuela were up front near the pilot and he had the back to himself. He thought, what an incredible lot of debris life leaves behind it as it goes wherever it was going. He took out his picture of the sailfish. Her eye seemed to stare at him sullenly, even inquisitively. Like, what will you do next? Maybe he would have one of the fiberglass mounts made exactly the size of the fish he had released. He'd hang it on the wall in his office. That way they could stare at each other

Sensualista

K irk arrived from San José on the little bush airstrip very early in the morning and there was no one to meet him. After flying over such a sea of green, the dusty strip was a bit of a letdown. Another lodge met the other visiting fishermen. When it was evident that he was going to be left standing, the guy said to hop aboard and he would drop him off at the phone office. As he was to discover, it was the only phone in town. A Canadian woman who sat there brushing off the flies gave a call to his fishing camp. The woman, who had a healthy good look, was in her early thirties and he wondered why in the world she would be living in this village where pigs fought over the latest garbage thrown out of the houses.

In a half hour or so a short, stocky man came up at a fast walk.

"Sorry there was no one here. I didn't know anyone was coming," and with that he heaved up Kirk's bags and off they walked to a small skiff tied at the river. On the way he remarked that the owner was forgetting more and more. "Plus he's got diabetes and is not supposed to drink."

Kirk thought it was a little strange to be confided in like this, but soon he was diverted by the hundreds of egrets wading and flying.

66

Occasionally they passed single cabins with dugouts for transportation. These cabins had no electricity, thus no blaring radios, only the shouts of numerous children.

His father, who had taught him what he knew of fishing, wanted them one day to fish for tarpon and billfish. That was impossible living in freshwater Missouri and it was a longstanding plan for the two of them to make these trips. While they were fishing for bass or catfish, his father talked about where they would go, what they would fish for.

This did not mean they did not enjoy what they were doing right then. Not at all. Whether it was cold or hot, whether they were lucky or not. Whether there was the new green of spring, or the changing fall colors. Whether watching a blue heron moving stealthily along the water's edge or the geese veeing their way north. Fishing for his father was a lifesaving change from his work as an attorney. His father felt that he was returning to a source of elemental energy, something that cleansed him.

Although he did combat in the courtroom, his father once said he would have preferred, perhaps, the combat of the animals that are beyond good and evil. On another occasion while they watched an osprey hover, then make off with a fish, he wondered if the osprey felt the beauty of the river as they did while they fished and looked on. Sometimes Kirk did not quite understand what his father was saying.

During Kirk's first year away from home and in college, his mother called to say his father had had a severe heart attack. Immediately he left for home and when he entered his father's room in intensive care after surgery, he was shocked at how much weight his father had lost. His face looked gaunt like a very premature baby's. Kirk was so moved, his eyes teared up as he leaned to kiss his father's cheek. He had not kissed his father since he was two or three years old.

Only his father's eyes could acknowledge Kirk was there. He was much sedated, and IVs and the probes of monitors were taped to his arms. It was a couple of days before he was alert enough to talk and even though his voice was weak, he brought up the trip they must make to Costa Rica where he had once fished. Kirk agreed, of course.

Two days later his father suffered a massive blockage during the night and he died. His mother was stoic during the following several days and before Kirk was to return to school, she sat with him in the garden. She told him that his father had said if he did not come through his illness, Kirk was to go on the fishing trip they had planned after his examinations.

As Kirk and the boatman worked their way up Rio Colorado, Kirk saw another lodge which had been advertised in the fishing magazines. It was carved out of a small place in the jungle, just as he was to find his own a mile or so upriver. The boatman tied up quickly and grabbed Kirk's bags and led the way to the first building which served as office, dining hall, and kitchen. The owner turned out to be a short man, ruddy from being in a lot of sun, with slightly bulging eyes which had some yellow in the whites. He apologized for the mixup. "No one had told me." Kirk gave him the paid bill he had received from the agent in San José.

He turned to the fellow with Kirk's bags. "Put him in number 7." Turning to Kirk, "As soon as you get stowed away, your guide will be waiting for you at the dock."

It was still only eight in the morning. Following the man with the bags he passed numerous tropical flowers that he did not recognize while overhead a flock of birds darted at great speed looking like white-winged dove but larger. At his question the man answered, "Parrots."

He was surprised how quickly he was to go fishing. In his half of a tin-roofed cabin, he emptied his bag on the spare bed and dressed in his fishing clothes. Back at the dock, Ramon, a wizened man of about forty, stood by one of the perhaps twenty skiffs that were tied up. They were eighteen to twenty feet in length with a beam of five feet. Nothing fancy. The outboard was started by hand and had a tiller. Kirk was to learn later that any mechanical part had to come from San Jose.

Back they traveled downriver from where Kirk had just come, but past the little village and the airstrip. Before they reached the river's mouth, Ramon pulled over to a shack that flew the Costa Rican flag. In front of the shack was a machine gun surrounded by sandbags about three feet high. It was official papers time. Ramon showed a wrinkled paper to one of the shabbily uniformed men. As Kirk was to realize after several days, these men saw the same boats day after day and they already knew Ramon. They all lived in the village. But it was government regulations. Or a way of being important, in lieu of a good salary. In turn they asked if Ramon had any ice and he said no but he would try to bring some tomorrow. So, a mild shakedown.

As the river broke out into the Caribbean, Kirk saw perhaps thirty boats, a virtual fleet of those who wanted to catch a tarpon, a fish that Kirk had read was a large member of the sardine family. Ramon cut the motor an appropriate distance from any nearby boat and handed him a rod and reel that was rigged with twenty-pound test and a hundred-pound shock leader. And the strangest lure Kirk had ever seen.

Ramon called it a Coast Hawk. It was about three inches long with two treble hooks. The body was made of solid metal. One end was thicker-bodied and had eyes painted on. Ramon told him to let it sink to the bottom, then reel up just a little. Bring the tip of the rod up and let the lure sink again. Kirk had fished jigs before, but this was the strangest jig he had ever seen. He saw other fishermen, though, moving their rod tips up and letting the lure fall. So he did the same.

After an hour of this there had been no action, plus Ramon was not very talkative.

Kirk ventured the question, "Do you ever troll for them?"

"Yes. I like trolling."

"Why don't we try that?"

Ramon tied on a six-and-a-half inch Rapala that was green on the top with black stripes and yellow on the bottom and on the other rod a five-inch Rapala, blue on top with a white bottom. Both lures had long lips to get them down. A yank on the cranking rope and they were moving north a few hundred feet offshore, Ramon holding one rod, Kirk the other.

For Kirk it was more opportunity to see the country. Occasionally small creeks would create dunes near their mouths. Eventually they came upon a small cargo ship that had broken on the beach. Ramon headed back south, a little further offshore, and wham, a tarpon parted the water in a leap and Kirk was hooked up with his very first. The fish was furious and jumped several more times, shaking and twisting his body above the water.

He kept pumping the rod and reeling the line back, all this from the board that served as a seat. There were no more jumps and the fish doggedly refused to come to the boat. Sweat soaked Kirk's shirt and pants and if a rare breeze happened by it was cool. After thirty minutes of this tug of war, while Ramon loafed in the back of the boat, another boat cut its engine and waited several hundred feet away. Two locals. They just sat there, looking on. Kirk thought that Ramon could have gaffed the fish several times before, but Ramon insisted it was too green, that it would tear the boat up. With his distant audience Kirk felt he had to go on. And on he went.

Finally the fish was exhausted. Ramon took the short gaff and jerked it through the lower jaw, pulling the big fish half way over the side.

"Can you take a picture?"

Ramon passed the gaff to Kirk who gave him the little camera. The fish was too big for Kirk to hold off the ground. Just then, the two men in the other boat came closer and yelled out something.

"They want to know if they can have the fish? I'll have to call the boss."

"What for? To eat?"

"Yes."

Kirk didn't think tarpon were good to eat. Because permission was granted, Kirk got his picture with the tarpon. The men ran the handle of the gaff through the large gill of the fish and held it up while he stood alongside.

On the way back for lunch, Ramon explained how the meat would be stripped from the carcass and made into balls, then fried. To the question of how much he thought the fish weighed, Ramon replied, "125."

Kirk was still dripping with sweat when he got back to the lodge and he felt drained. Lunch was already on the buffet table, but he couldn't eat much and simply drank a lot of juice. Mostly he wanted to strip off his clothes and lie on the bed until two o'clock when he would go out again. As he left the dining room he again heard coughing, this time from a small office off the dining room. He fell asleep under a ceiling fan thinking about his father.

The fan's breeze made him a little stiff when he got up but as they headed back out to sea, he once again, like all fishermen, looked forward to being surprised by what would hit his line and emerge from the water. There was still a small fleet of boats where the water of the river flowed into the sea, but Ramon turned the boat north again and Kirk let out his line. Almost immediately something powerful hit his deep-swimming lure and he waited for the powerful jump of the tarpon but nothing happened. Whatever it was reeled off line and when he pumped the rod and tried to get some back, it was a tussle.

Ramon said, "Jack."

Kirk had not caught a jack and did not know what one was. After fifteen minutes he finally saw the silvery, flat tall body and could see how such a fish, though only twenty inches long, could get such torque in the water. Like a big freshwater sunfish. Ramon whacked the fish with a club, unhooked him, and they began again only to hook another one.

"Maybe we should go back near the other boats."

"Fine," agreed a tiring Kirk. So it was back to jigging the Coast Hawk.

Once they had anchored, Kirk realized that one advantage in being here was seeing others hook tarpon and all the whooping and hollering that came with it.

More volume was added by those who had brought lots of beer with them.

Once Kirk jigged the Coast Hawk so he could see its action near the boat, he decided it looked like a squid, at least perhaps to a tarpon. Soon he was hooked up to one who had been fooled. Again the great silvery leaps. This time he thought he fished better. Ramon had told him that when the tarpon leaped, he should point the rod at him, or bow to him, giving immediate slack to the line so he would not break it above the leader.

After the leaps came the hard work of bringing him in, always working the rod against the direction the fish wanted to go in order to tire him quickly. The fish did come in quicker than the morning tarpon. One reason was he was smaller, perhaps sixty pounds. At this point in the day Kirk thought he enjoyed the smaller one. In the skiff there was no helpful fighting chair like he had seen in fishing magazines. He could stand, or sit on the board seat. Kirk was again fascinated by the fish's seemingly bottomless dark eye.

Some of the other boats had already cranked up and headed back. "Can we get a picture?"

"He is too green. He would tear the boat up if he got loose."

Kirk was beginning to think Ramon was a bum.

After releasing the fish Ramon asked if he was ready to go and Kirk agreed. The tide was running in and as it met the outflowing river there were rollers they ploughed through four or five feet high. During the trip back, Ramon happened to mention that his daughter was helping in the kitchen, that he would wait until after supper in order to bring her home.

Kirk took his personal bag to his cabin and reveled in the shower. He appreciated the difficulty of having hot water and the generators for electricity in the middle of the bush like this. There were no roads to the lodge.

After he put on fresh shorts and shirt, he crossed the garden to a small building connected by a breezeway to where the bar was where all the other fishermen, some ten or twelve, were drinking and talking. No one introduced himself but listening to everyone, he discovered everyone had had good luck. A fly fisherman had kept a large tarpon on for a long time but lost him finally.

The first cold beer was magic and seemed a reward for the hard fishing.

Three of the men were airline pilots. One of them was telling about hunting leopard in Africa. He and his guide sat in a blind waiting for one (which finally he killed), but what caught Kirk's attention was the guide telling the hunter, "Whatever happens, don't cough. The leopard will think it's another leopard and come bounding over to our blind, ready to take on the competition."

Just then the owner came in with a couple of plates of paper-thin slices of tuna with Japanese hot mustard called wasabi, putting one on the table where the pilots were and one where Kirk and others were. The owner remarked to the pilots' table he had a lot of frequent-flyer miles going to San José and to a famous bar called the Sailfish (which they all seemed to know was a whorehouse, too) and the pilot who had shot the leopard said, "Well, one thing I know, I've got more mileage on my dick than you have."

Everyone laughed, including Kirk though he was hiding a little embarrassment at the crudeness, and the owner went from laughing to the hacking rattle of coughing.

Several beers later they all filed into the dining room. The salads and vegetables were on the buffet, but one went to the counter of the kitchen for either steak or freshly sautéed fish fillets. That is when Kirk saw, besides the big jolly black woman who ran the kitchen, Ramon's daughter. She was perhaps sixteen, and both were soon flirting with each other. She was smoking a cigarette awkwardly, clearly for the first few times. Kirk was the only one in the dining room who was close to her age.

After the beers and dinner, tiredness settled fast on Kirk and he was glad to go to bed. In addition, a light rain began to fall on the tin roof. He fell asleep but it wasn't long before he heard an animal squall and he thought it was a jaguar, because there had been talk about them. The black-and-tan ten-month-old puppy that the owner had brought down from Florida was trailing him and howling intermittently. Kirk would like to have seen him, but he wasn't stepping outside the cabin.

He drifted in and out of uneasy sleep, sometimes seeing the dark eye of the tarpon, hearing the squalling of the big cat, the howling of the black-and-tan or the coughing of the owner.

He went early to the dining room because a pot of coffee was always there even though breakfast was not yet started. He took his cup outside to the shed where the guides normally congregated. Several others had the same idea, including the pilots. Two of them were complaining about their hangovers. Soon guides began coming in and tying up their boats.

Kirk spotted Ramon at the tiller of one and the girl in the bow seat. While Ramon tied up and began arranging tackle, she walked swinging her small hips in her jeans toward the kitchen. She did not look at Kirk or any of the men. The pilot with such great mileage made a guttural sound somewhat like a baboon, accompanied by his buddies' chuckling. Kirk flushed, embarrassed for her.

Ramon turned south this time and they began trolling. The sea was slick at first but soon began to heave. Kirk could a see an isolated rainstorm, surrounded by sunshine. There were no life jackets on the boat. On the beach a solitary dog played, far from any village.

As Kirk headed out to sea he thought how different fishing with his father had been from fishing around this so-called international sporting set. It seemed to him that some of these men had blunted their senses, or at least they talked that way. Just like the way they talked about women and sex. Kind of a spiritless game. Maybe he was too inexperienced. As he mulled this over, he thought too of Ramon's daughter. Maybe he could talk to her.

A Fox Hunt

I t was Saturday and cold. The load we took to the stockyard
brought good prices, and Bo and I were both feeling good. I was
feeling the best, because every load was another bite against the
mortgaged herd. The auction itself was lively, and the smell of cows
and wood shavings made us feel comfortable. But when we started
back, there was thick traffic near the chemical plants. Sometimes in
traffic Bo's mean streak showed through as he bullied the road with
the big truck. He controlled himself today and didn't run anyone off
the shoulder; but the plants offended us—especially the oily smells.

We stopped at the last bar in the ward, and I went in and got two
bottles of beer and two hot sausages. It would be more than twenty-
five miles before the next bar. There were several dry wards, and
sometimes we would stop even if we weren't thirsty. But today we
were. The first few cold days had heightened our senses; the leaves
were greener, the air clearer.

The hot juicy beef sausages warmed our insides as we ate. When
the pleasant burning became a little too hot, we swallowed cold beer.

"Man-o-man, I believe this is here to stay," said Bo, eating the
sausage with his left hand, the beer leaning precariously against the

back of the seat, and shifting the big truck and steering with the other hand.

As the miles rolled by, the country changed to small well-kept pastures and fields. Many of the small farms were owned by the men in the plants who did this as a hobby—fellows who decided they really wouldn't try to make a living from farming, but just wanted to be around cows and cornfields. Their farms looked better than the bigger ones where we lived, but they didn't make any money. The permanent pastures were yellow and brown, but now and then the bright emerald of ryegrass or oats passed in sudden contrast.

"Well, shot, what do you have lined up this afternoon? Gettin' into trouble or something to further your interests?" Bo had not turned to speak, but was looking a little to the left at the rolling country, broken by patches of pine woods.

I knew what was on his mind, and it was on mine too. "No, I ain't got nothing special planned."

The drone, drone of the truck on the pavement.

"Those hounds are gonna get soft feet if we don't run 'em pretty soon," he said, matter-of-factly.

"Yeah, I guess so," as if it didn't really matter, but it did. I was glad. But the thing about soft feet. It was true that hounds had to be run regularly if their feet were to stay hard—Bo had taught me that—but he acted like that was the only reason he was interested in running hounds sometimes. And as if it was a favor to me, most of the time.

It was supposed to be as a favor to me that I now had dogs. As fall came on, Mr. Tillman had gone mad (from constricting arteries, the doctors said) and had had to go to the geriatric hospital at the asylum. All his dogs needed somebody to take care of them, and Bo asked if I was interested. He even hinted that Mr. Tillman might not be able to come back for a long, long time and that I could just as well see them as my dogs. Of course, *I* probably couldn't get the dogs, but *he* would ask the old man and say *he* was taking care of them, and it would be all right. I'd been wanting a pack of hounds bad and so replied "hell yes" I would take care of them. It also turned out that Bo became a "caretaker" for Mr. Tillman's land. Leave it to Bo to figure an angle.

So even though the dogs were called Bo's (Bo not actually claim-ing an outright share because he would place himself liable for part of the feed bill of twenty-one hounds, though in fact he fed them as much as I did, maybe more, and certainly doctored them altogether), they were in fact mine. But he knew about hounds like he knew about cows, and I listened to him in all things. Even from the few hunts I had made, I could understand that running red fox was not really for boys or for fun. There was probably more fun in running rabbits or coon. I had done that. Running fox was another kind of thing. Sometimes you cast the dogs and there was nothing, not even a whimper. Somewhere, of course, there probably was a race, but by the time the hounds struck, they were too far away. Or you knew they were running a fox, but he was in a place where you couldn't get close.

"We ought to try and turn out sometime after four or five if we can, so he'll be stinkin' good before dark," said Bo. He had explained before that once the fox ran for an hour or two, it was much easier for the hounds to trail him because his "stink machine" was putting out so much musk. I believe I even smelled it myself once, but, then, I knew he had crossed.

"Ruth's been asking to go hunting the next time we go. Be all right to bring her along?"

"Sure. Glad to have her," he replied, and in a way that I knew he meant it. Because this wasn't a woman's thing. Bo didn't ever want his wife along. I think that's why he got the dogs, just so he could have a reason to stay out of the house now that I had all of his cows. When he disappeared mysteriously for a couple of days, he came back with nothing to do. With the same businesslike attitude that he had with the cows, he turned to doctoring the dogs and getting them in running condition after they had lain around Mr. Tillman's place. It was either right or not at all.

"If you'd like to make a little party of it, we could invite Mr. Cy and his dogs. I understand he's picked up a bitch out of Arkansas that will mortally tear a fox's ass up."

"Where you figure a good place to turn out'll be?

"I've been seeing good signs over in Miss Ida's place, down near that little wooden bridge." Miss Ida was an old widow that lived way back in the woods in the middle of good casting grounds—her husband having left her a thousand acres (among other things) which she seldom came out of. When she did, she came in an old Chrysler about ninety miles an hour, swerving from one shoulder of the road to the other, scaring chickens, guineas, and black children who all, together, jumped into the ditch or tried to scratch their way through or over the nearest fence.

"I sure hope we hear a race tonight, with Ruth coming and all," I said.

"You don't have to worry about *hope* tonight, I don't believe, because the ground's gonna be real dewy and it'll be real still," he said emphatically. We passed our own parish line, and far up the road I saw the sign advertising Tuck's bar.

"After we get to your place, I'll get the pickup and come back to Tuck's and fill up the box with beer and groceries. I'll need to call Ruth at the asylum and tell her what time to be ready. Meet you at my place at four."

"I'll send word to Mr. Cy, and if he comes, we'll all meet at your place." Mr. Cy Freeman didn't have a phone, and a younger drinking buddy of his would have to tell him. He lived up in Mississippi and could come down in the daylight, but he couldn't drive at night because his left eye was out and he couldn't see well enough to go home afterward. A fighting chicken had struck him somehow with the metal gaff it wore in the pit.

We came to Bo's place, and I took off in the pickup for Tuck's to call Ruth. I didn't really want to have to go in with Bo to talk to his wife. Whatever there was, was between him and me. His wife was another world. She was loyal to Bo, but as if she had learned fidelity from the Catholic Church. She was just Bo's woman, like a squaw. Not that this was the way Bo looked at her—or not *only* this way. There was something I hadn't figured out yet about them. He held her up on a pedestal because she didn't drink or smoke or do the mysterious work Bo did for the Teamsters when he would disappear. She stayed home and raised children and went to church. But she wasn't a farm woman. She didn't even go outside unless it was to go to town to the store. That, and she also kept the books for Bo.

She was never in open opposition to Bo. He wouldn't have that. But she was like a nagging mosquito in a bedroom. Even though it hasn't downright bit you, it's there. It's aggravation. This woman was aggravation. She knew how to purse her lips when Bo would say he was going hunting, knew how to raise her forehead in a slight wrinkle, just a little wrinkle, if he was going off with me, for that might mean he was going to have a beer or two. It's the snake in the woods you can't see that spooks you the most.

The old blue pickup was mine, now. Bo's truck. It, too, was on his books. I had made my six-month payment on the herd, but all the little things added up, the truck, the hay. It did have a way of adding up.

But on a crisp, cold day in the fall, it's hard to study on such things. I had built an icebox in the back of the truck, next to the cab. It would hold about two cases of beer and left a little room for cheese, sausage, and such on a top tray.

I told Tuck to get me the two cases and I used his phone to call Ruth. She had just gotten off duty and her voice sounded excited. She didn't have to work the next day either. I told her the hunt could last all night.

"Looks like you planning a real party," said Tuck as I returned from the phone.

"Yeah, believe we might get warmed up tonight. Maybe you better give me one Heineken's for the road, Tuck."

"You must be feeling good," he cackled, bringing the bright green bottle of Dutch beer to me. "Any time you spring loose with money." The Heineken cost twice as much as the regular beer.

With the first bitter-good taste of the strange beer, I felt like staying there awhile, but I knew I had to keep moving to pick up Ruth in time. What was holding me was a little fire in Tuck's big fireplace, just enough during the daytime if you backed up to it.

Through the window, the sky was still cloudless, and there was scarcely a ripple on the surface of the lake. It was bound to be a good running night, or I hoped hard that it would be. I felt very happy. I even thought about the people who made Heineken's beer and hoped they had a good fire, too. I doubted whether they had a good pack of foxhounds, but maybe they had something else just as good. I felt very noble and generous in thinking such a thing, which made me feel even better.

"Tuck, you are certainly a great tavern keeper. This is our sanctuary by the road of life." It seemed fitting to be bombastic and wise today. He looked at me with a jaundiced eye and as if he might also call the asylum.

Then he said, "Yes, that is very true."

Having settled most of the major mysteries, I got up and took one of the cases of beer, and Tuck helped me with the other one. I placed the bottles of one case in the bottom, got a bag of ice and covered them, then did the same with the other case.

About this time Jo Anne, a nutty friend of mine, drove up about ninety miles an hour, swirling up dust as she stopped. Tuck was on his way back toward the bar and I was in the truck as she got out. I waved but kept going. She looked a little disappointed, but I didn't have time for her this day.

Ruth came out of the nurses' quarters before I got to the door. She had on blue jeans and a dark gray pullover sweater, and she carried a denim jacket flung over her shoulder. Her long dark hair shone in the bright sunlight and looked richer because of the deep red lipstick she wore.

"So I'm finally getting to go, huh?" she smiled.

"We'll have a fine night if the wind doesn't pick up," I said, helping her into the truck. "Bo is going to ask an old man from Mississippi, Mr. Cy Freeman, if he wants to bring his dogs, and if he does, it'll be something if they all get on the same fox. Hope so, but you know that maybe we won't hear a thing. That's usually the way it turns out. Then we just stay out in the woods all night for nothing."

"It won't matter. I'm glad to get away from the hospital."

I guess being in an asylum is not supposed to be happy hour, no matter how many pretty flowers are planted or what shape the buildings are—but that place gave me the dirty willies. The nurses' quarters had once been a big plantation home, but now it was just tacky. Too many separate entrances and walkways had to be built to make it efficient. It probably would have been much more expensive to tear it down and start over. The new one-story buildings where the patients lived probably were pretty enough just after the state had built them, but the same bums hanging out at Dud Dickly's bar near the asylum were taking care of things, and even these buildings were beginning to look like an old World War II airbase that wasn't used any more. Dark rusty water stains, the color of an old smoker's fingers, daggered the concrete walls.

Around Ruth's eyes was a little tiredness that disappeared as she laughed at a battered RC Cola sign we had both laughed at before. It had been peppered by rifle shots a long time ago, the holes making their ironic comment on *Skinnerville, Where the Charm of the Old South Still Lives.* At the base of the sign were the broken bottles thrown by Skinnerville's finest marksmen from their fast-moving cars.

By the time we came to my house, the sun was already losing its little heat and light. There were some hot coals still in the fireplace, and I threw a few little pieces on for Ruth to get warm by. No use building much of a fire, with Bo and Mr. Cy coming along soon.

I poured her a little glass of whiskey because she didn't like to drink much beer. After she took the first sip of whiskey and settled back in her rocking chair, she seemed to loosen up all over. She looked into the new flames. "Two patients died today, and one of them was really kind of a buddy."

"What happened to them?"

"They just died in their sleep. Both of them had been sick for a while from the flu."

Being around the sick and the dead does odd things to good-looking women. I had seen it in the Army hospitals before, with women that had all the parts of good bodies and faces. But somehow having to empty the bedpans and touch the sick flesh—just being always in the presence of people as meat and fluids—this kept them from seeming romantic. Or maybe just from seeming that way to me. They were deprived of the right to be frank, temptress-sirens. And Ruth, even in her blue jeans and sweater, carried with her the sense of the sick and the dead, which sat awkwardly on such eyes.

I said cleverly, "Drink your whiskey," and she did.

Bo drove up with the older man right back of him. Mr. Cy was seventy-three and could still drink all day and night, Bo said. He might wheeze a little the next morning because of some lung trouble. Women up around where he lived said his drinking was going to kill him and that it had caused his lung trouble. These were the widow women he might still take a turn with, but who were mostly in their fat fifties.

I stepped out on the porch and greeted him.

"Howdy, son." We shook hands and just then Ruth stepped through the doorway. The old man's face became suddenly impassive, but his one eye was riveted on her. She fit her denim pants snugly, and her figure was held in outline by the light of the house at her back.

"Mr. Cy, I'd like for you to meet Ruth Coleman."

"How do you do, sir."

"How do you do, ma'am," each respectful of the other.

Bo spoke then. "Well, let's load up ours, podnuh. Looks like those mongrels of Mr. Cy's are all ready to go," and started for the gap to let it down for me to drive through. Ruth stayed back with the old man, both sitting on the porch.

Loading the dogs was a wild circus. All the hounds were in two dog yards, side by side, and when the truck with the dog crate was backed up, nearly every hound in the house came rushing up to the gate. Since they lazed around all day with nothing to do, the older ones had to stretch and yawn first, but the young ones just scampered over. Bo excited them even more with whistles and shouts, like he was urging them on already, and they leaped up and yelped.

I stood by the dog crate and grabbed whatever Bo would hand me, and he handed me whatever he could grab in a wild melee of eager dogs all wanting to catch a trail at the entrance. There really was a fox in a thicket right back of the dog yard, but he was an old gray who knew how to run up a tree after fifteen minutes.

Bo was quicker to reveal his cruel streak when animals didn't do his bidding. As one young hound tried to sneak past him the second time, he gave it a boot, yelling, "You son of a bitch!" Which was appropriate on the one hand, but sent the dog screaming back to the doghouse where one other hound that we called Skittish Bitch remained.

After we had loaded everything else, Bo yelled to the hound he had kicked, "Come out of there, you bastard." The hound wasn't moving.

"He ain't no fool," I piped up, but Bo ignored me and snatched him out of the house by his collar. He was gentler with the bitch, who had in the few weeks since we got her become a kind of prima donna. But temperamental or not, she could run right up at the front.

When we drove back to the porch, Ruth and Mr. Cy were deep in conversation, so Bo hollered out that he would drive with me, and she could go in the other truck. We led the way back to Miss Ida's fields, not going by the front where her house was, but coming in by a road in the back. I didn't know whether Bo had ever asked her if he could hunt on her property. Most people didn't care, and most hunters never asked. And there was no point in giving her the chance to refuse.

When we came to a slough at the edge of a meadow, we stopped and got out. Bo walked back to Mr. Cy as he drew up and asked him if he would like to turn out first; but he said no thanks, since this was our stomping grounds, we could find the fox. Bo then suggested, "Well, maybe you might want to lend a hand with the Arkansas bitch."

"All right. If that's the case."

The etiquette was a little complex here. This was our running territory. Hunters rarely went into other folks' territory unless they were invited. The violation was handled in several ways other than just a fistfight or shotguns. The neatest way was to turn out your dogs after theirs had got the fox up running. Most hunters want to hear their dogs and not something they hadn't been feeding. This solution was especially good when you had dogs that could take the fox away from theirs. If you didn't have good dogs, the next best thing was to have a dog that could start a fight. Normally fox hunters didn't stoop to using cur dogs for this but rather a hound that had developed this habit. Most hounds weren't interested in fighting—just running.

Mr. Cy was a guest. Guests generally insisted the host turn out first. But Mr. Cy was older than us—that was an important consid-

eration. All of this sounds complicated, I guess, like Korean etiquette. Explaining it sounds too complicated for us to have cared
about. But it was all there—there in the deep, gray-blue twilight of
a dying fall day.

Mr. Cy felt around in the squirming dogdom of his crate and
called for Arkansas—"Miss Arkansas." She finally came to the gate,
and he brought her out holding her collar while she trembled on the
ground by the truck and the strangers.

There were no choices as we opened our gate. Bo stepped out in
the direction of the slough and said, "All right." I opened it, feeling
there was a mighty power I was about to let loose in Cypress Parish
on an October night. Bang. Scrambling. Fighting for the opening,
surging to the clapping hands and "heah, heah" of Bo.

Then Mr. Cy silently released his bitch, who joined the strange
dogs, knowing what there was to do. Once the dogs started in the
right direction, Bo came back, but nobody spoke—only listened. It
was like a great sound stage with "On the Air" lighted—quiet, cold
quiet, electric—like we had told the woods and the wind to halt, to
wait just one minute while we prepared. Every head bowed, every
eye closed.

Then like a high-school soprano cracking the gulf after a Baptist
prayer, the long high mouth of the Skittish Bitch had attacked the
first fox code, the red-stink mystery of the night. Simmons' nose
was up like he was sniffing the air, the creases from his eyes and
forehead gone. Then again. "Hooohhh." Now a little quicker.
Finally a horn-mouth dog named Blaze let sing like he would
never take a breath, and they alternated down the slough, around
the meadow.

For a moment they shut up. Ruth spoke for the first time, asking,
"What are they doing now? They quit barking."

"They lost it just a second. They'll get it again," Bo explained,
with great confidence. "Might've hit a patch of water."

"And, Ruth," I said, "not *barking*—singing. Giving a lot of mouth,
giving tongue—but not barking."

"Well, excuse me."

"Ruth," Mr. Cy explained more patiently, "they are 'cold trailing' now. The fox has been there where they whoop once in a while. He's been looking for bugs and rats to eat. It's early and he hasn't been walking around much. He already knows they're after him. He'll light out, and if they don't lose his cold trail, they'll hump him. Then all the dogs will start whooping. All those that can keep up, anyway," he grinned.

Bo laughed appreciatively. Some of our dogs weren't really up to snuff and he knew it. But we had to keep them all for Mr. Tillman.

Finally a scream, like pain. "Somebody lit a firecracker under that one," exclaimed Bo, jumping around and wringing his hands together. "Believe I better have another beer."

There were two bitches of ours, Dolly and Pearl, that had what we called crying mouths, and they opened up. The first time I had heard them, I thought they really were crying. Those mouths I liked the best—those and the horn mouth, the long drawn-out one like Blaze. Bo liked a steady, relentless, chopping mouth like our Bawlin' dog. Just a steady "Aww, Aww, Aww."

But in the beginning they were all there, hot and happy, and at least Ruth was getting to see and hear this—this thing that I'd learned to enjoy more than most any other thing, more even than fooling with cows, or rocking in a chair on a porch in the rain. And certainly rain on a tin roof will compete with most things a man does. But this was a special excitement, after a red fox, feeling that at last you were about to pursue him—it—a runner you mostly never saw.

"You never shoot a fox?" Ruth asked.

"Oh, no!" answered Bo. "We might bring some more into the country, or pay niggers to raise chickens so they might have something to eat, but not kill 'em."

When I had asked Bo to go squirrel hunting one day, he had said, "Hoss, I just lost my interest in gun hunting. Don't get me wrong, I used to love to do it. I've killed so many quail in one day that we had to carry 'em home in croaker sacks. Dove the same way. I've even shot three deer in one day. But I just got tired of it. I just let the dogs do it for me now." I knew he could shoot. I had been practicing one day with a twenty-two rifle my grandpa had left in the closet—shooting off the porch at anything I could see, and I passed the gun to Bo, who acted like it was a strange thing in his hand, the way he looked at it. But when he shot a beer can way off against a bank of dirt, I couldn't believe it. He was good at shooting, but he never went gun hunting. Just lost interest. Not me, though.

No, Ruth, we don't shoot the fox, because then what would we pursue? Even do? Would we leave and go have a drink? The fox takes us out of ourselves, and drinking is a much greater thing in the woods. It is clean and uplifting in a way it could never be in a bar-room. You go *there* to rest. But in the woods and after the fox there is no rest. Even if the hounds have lost the scent and the fox has lost himself in a hole. There is waiting for some hound, somewhere still looking, still smelling for that sweet puzzle that transforms it from the laziest-looking mutt that might or might not scratch itself, to a charging, traveling, red-eyed hunter. And only the bright clear day-light might stop the hunt, the pursuit—maybe so we can all rest up for the next dark time.

The pack made it around the meadow once, then twice, then like a rock twirled from an Old Testament slingshot, zoomed off in a straight line, still in hearing distance, but growing faint. Bo said, "Mr. Cy, you want to take a spin around the road, just to be sure they don't go out of hearing? Farley can stay here with Ruth unless they stay out of hearing." Then, turning to me, "You can meet us up by that old blown-down shack at the top of Turner's Hill. I know they can't be out of hearing there."

Mr. Cy got in his truck and took Bo with him. "We'll probably be right back," said Bo. "I just want to be sure we don't lose that bugger."

Without the presence of the other two men, suddenly, there was the immense aloneness of dark silence. The insect world was gone with the cold, and the hounds were faint enough to be ignored if you didn't strain. I got us some crackers and cheese, and Ruth even took a beer. We sat on the dog crate side by side and bingo: another moment to make all the effort worth living for, to be separated from bending your back for a foreman or hacking it under a platoon ser-geant with half a brain. I knew this moment was good and that I didn't have to be gone from it five years in order to moan about the good old days. Now, now is the time for all laddies to come to the aid of their lassies. So I leaned over in celebration and, fighting the coldness, held bonny Ruth close and kissed her beer-moistened lips, those full and voluptuous portals of fiery spine chills. Home!

Yes, what fox? Fox hunt? The next thing I knew, the hounds were roaring by like the devil unleashed and I hadn't even heard them come, busy with other pounding in my ears, another pursuit.

Then they returned, clambering back to us. This time we didn't miss the building power, the sweep guidoned by a doubtless red beauty, and our own flight was boosted, elevated by love and booze. Oh, King Henry from across the sea, eat your heart out! Flying, floating, red skin, tipped tail flying, with canines trying to bite the ass out of lightning.

"Ain't that sumpin'! You hear it? *Did you hear it?*" from Bo. As if he wanted to hear it all, cupping it (the din, the howlwind roar) all in his ear for lasting time, the last time.

"Yes, we heard."

"Oh, Mr. Cy, isn't it grand?" asked Ruth—this question to an old man who had heard so many, many cries and choruses crowning the hills of southern Mississippi like the heavenly Gabriels for a lesser garden (what could be greater than our garden?).

"Yes ma'am. It is that, all right." Him hearing the female yes, maybe (I imagined) for the first time, because in his time, chasing red ghosts through piney woods was no affair for a "lady." Ladies change, don't they, Mr. Cy? Ain't this a lady, Mr. Cy? She, beautiful and sportin', who can be kind and respectful, yet drink with you drink for drink (almost) on a cold night, drink the hound glory and fox fire, but not tag you with: "Cyrus! Time to get up and feed. Get up, Cyrus. If you wouldn't lie out all night you would amount to somethin'" (I imagined). No, Mr. Cy. Your wife is in the cold, cold ground, and you are hung to a flying-ghost squad (you cannot part from them without a failure in faith).

They headed now around the meadow again, past the place where they had jumped, then were off like a shot before making a gentle swing back.

"I think we're in the right place," confirmed Bo, and lit a match from a package he carried only when he went hunting at night. He did not smoke tobacco of any kind, hated it, so never had a need for matches.

He pushed some leaves together under the twigs and lit the little pile and blew on them like a cherub in the old illustrated Bibles, cheeks puffed out, trying to light the fire of the world. And the glow of life was there from our redneck wind man.

He went dancing off in the woods to bring back long branches of hardwood. Then he stood about three feet from one end and cracked off the other. Pile 'em on.

"Don't let that truck keep you from helping now, hoss," Bo admonished me. "Those dogs'll be making circles here all night long. Bank on it." So I stumbled into the cold darkness to bring its own destruction back with me. Chunks big as watermelons, with logs to sit on.

And the bell-mouth hounds, FBI to errant foxes, sang through their tree-trunk world, knowing (I like to think) what they were trying to catch. The sweet smell of success. Is it really only the way you play the game?

There we were: an old man and two young folks with a middle-man in between, hunched on logs with fire in our eyes, even when we turned to the darkness. The hounds were at a far turn when Bo showed Ruth how to cup her hand behind her ear. She jumped with surprise as the sound roared in because of this new magic.

For a while they seemed to hole up in a spot on the other side of the meadow, like they were in a brier patch, or maybe they were going to drive him up a tree.

Bo and Mr. Cy again moved off to get closer to the fox, and I moved close to Ruth. The chase, I began to understand, was not homogeneous with woman. Nor she with it. It was as if, as Ruth turned to me, there was no race—almost. She was a lot of woman, meaning: ignoring the whoop and holler of run, her long-ago mothers had cooked by fires like this and heard the chorus of men and dogs in the distance, finally just believing that "all this maleness has gotten us this far, and who knows what tomorrow may bring. I will think about the fire and the pot and this place. Let them go where they will, as long as they come back."

Now the fire had its coals. We moved our log back to keep from burning our legs when our pants heated up and we shifted. Bo and Mr. Cy came back then, and we settled down. The hounds knew their fox, and the fox knew just how fast he had to run to stay out of reach. Sometimes, as if perhaps to get a breather, he would tear off in an orbit that stretched out of hearing ten or fifteen minutes, only then to return to circles and parabolas that had us and a fire as a center—almost as if we were the generating hub, the centrifugal force that spun the fox's music around our head, instead of just the other way around. It, they, the fox and the hounds, created their own circle and center.

The red ghost glided, sifted through the black bramble world outside our firelight because (I like to think) of his own choosing. This was maybe morality or beauty to a fox, to run or not to run. They knew they could run up a tree and be safe, or down a hole. And some foxes did take the easy out.

The dogs were not interested in devouring the fox. They just had to believe they were for the moment. After they caught one, which they rarely did, they left it. Bo said he had once put one in a dog crate and they didn't even bother it. It was the pursuit that counted.

Ruth started to doze, and Mr. Cy went to his truck and brought back two or three croaker sacks. "Here, young lady. Curl up by the fire and sleep when you feel like it," smoothing them out in front of the log. She grinned as if she had been defeated by sleep, and lay down with one sack over her. And probably for the first time in his life the old man had a woman to share his fire in the woods.

During the night as even I dozed, I awoke to see Bo, who never went to sleep, throw a beam of light out in the darkness as if he always knew where the demon was, and there, in red-running fire, it was. Not a phantom or a dream, but a real fox.

Late Hookup

The struggle had started near sundown. Now it was midnight and Mark, the older man, could not see an end to it. Long ago he should have said something. After all, he was the one paying the guide. He had worked the big tarpon for an hour, then handed the rod to Eddie. In the last several years he had caught many big tarpon, especially in Costa Rica. But now he had many things wrong within his chest and stomach. Straining for hours was no longer the smart thing to do. Yet he still loved to see the silver fish hurl itself into the air. Mostly though the beauty was brief, then the long grind. Like some other trajectories.

During the morning of yesterday, the first day of fishing, they had caught snook. South Florida was famous for its snook. Not only was the snook a fine game fish with plenty of action, but it was also very good to eat. Because it was good to eat and fished so heavily, the season was sometimes closed. No matter what time of the year it was, though, it did not matter to Mark because he fished for the fun of it. He had never been interested in fishing for records. Being on the water and in the mangroves was just a place for reflection, or for not thinking at all. One small redfish or speckled trout was enough for a meal if he decided to eat one, otherwise he turned them loose.

It was while chatting in the boat yesterday that he began to learn about his guide. Mark had noticed what looked like surgery on Eddie's face, but of course he had not asked him about it. Eddie was short, massively built with the obligatory tough-guy tattoos on his arms. He had not been guiding long, although he knew the waters very well. Previously a stone crabber, his fortunes fell with a steep decline in the crabs. In order not to lose his boat, he started moving dope from the mother ships that waited offshore with their loads from Colombia. He was bitter about being caught and losing his boat. Still, back when it happened, the sentence for marijuana was not long. It was long enough though to get his face carved up by some Mexicans who were sharing the prison with him. The scars caused his face to look twisted and even menacing whether he tried to smile, which was not often, or was frustrated. From the drift of the conversation, Eddie felt guiding was a big step down from running his own crab boat.

After they finished fishing for snook, Eddie caught some large mullet with his cast net and they went a short distance up a mangrove river and anchored. The falling tide would bring many baitfish and this would attract tarpon. Not long after hooking two mullet through their lips and letting them freeline, a tarpon did hit very quickly, but he missed the bait. Perhaps the tarpon was distracted, for a shark hit him immediately.

There were many sharks about, creating problems if you were fishing for tarpon. Still it was a beautiful dread to see a big shark moving fast on the bait of mullet as he pulled the line in panic. The sharks pushed through the water like barely submerged submarines. Twice the two men had reeled in quickly to avoid a hookup. Finally a shark that was not seen swallowed the circle hook and the point dug in for good. Mark began to work him, but the reels they were using did not hold much line. The line was far into the backing before Eddie, cursing all the way, could get the motor started.

Eddie yelled at him, "You gotta tell me when you're in the backing." Soon they were racing after him, getting most of the line back, then as he got closer to the boat he streaked toward the sea, ripping off line like a huge, fantasy bonefish. Again and again they did this. As he worked the shark, Mark thought about the guide yelling at him and he didn't care for it much.

Eddie said several times, "He'll break off any minute." The leader was monofilament. If one was going after sharks he used a wire leader. After two hours he still had not broken it. They both wanted to see how big he was and just before dark he came close enough to see. A brawny eight-foot Bull shark. He shook his head in a fury and finally broke the leader. It was too late to bait up again for the tarpon. There was nothing to do about it.

"We'll get tarpon tomorrow," remarked Eddie. Mark had previously told him he would fish for two days, after which he had several hundred miles to drive the following morning. For a moment he thought about canceling tomorrow's fishing, for he was still annoyed about being yelled at. But, as he sipped on a cold beer during the trip back through the evening air and the mangroves, he forgot about it.

Late the next afternoon found them in the river again. Eddie again netted some big mullet and they anchored for the outgoing tide. At first it seemed barely to move but as the tide increased it swept through the mangrove roots sounding like a mountain stream. There came with it a storm of bait as it picked up speed. Flurries of finger mullet over a nearby shoal flung themselves into the air fleeing something bigger than they were. Mark thought he could feel the river taut with the coming frenzy of fish hunting fish, a lunging feast of striking and killing. For an hour or so there was no action except twice they had reeled in their lines to avoid sharks. The sun was not far from going down.

They both had seen tarpon rolling some distance from where they were, and one of the largest mullet was cast far upstream above a slight bend in order for it to sweep by that spot. Suddenly a big one launched himself into the air. For a moment Mark didn't know if the fish was on his line or not, but that question was answered quickly. The fish streaked toward the open sea, peeling off line as Eddie reeled his line in and hurriedly pulled up the anchor and started the engine.

"Reel fast, reel fast," he ordered.

Mark was already reeling in easily for the boat was moving rapidly with the fish. He thought his guide must not be used to this. He seemed agitated. One of the problems was his guide had not brought reels large enough to hold 300 yards of line. With just 100 yards, naturally a big tarpon could quickly strip it. When the fish would decide to make a run, Eddie had to scramble to crank up and chase him. During these times the fish was not being whipped down by forcing the rod and line against the way the fish wanted to go.

Another consequence of the chases was they were now in the open sea. No longer was the small boat protected by the mangroves and then night caught up with them. Mark didn't feel there was much point in going on because they could not even see the fish. He mentioned this.

"I got a new spotlight." He raised a seat lid and came out with one still in the hard plastic package. He put the engine in neutral and tried hooking the leads to one of the batteries. No light. He began to fool with various connections, then the tarpon decided he wanted to go elsewhere. In a few minutes they stopped and he kept trying to get his new, cheap spotlight to work. He sprinkled his efforts with frustrated cursing.

"You want to head in?"

"Ah, we'll get this sonofabitch. He may be a record."

Mark thought, "I don't need a record." He thought too about having to drive all the next day.

"I tell you what. Why don't you try your hand at this?"

"You bet. You can run the motor. I'd like to see how big this bastard is. We can take him back to the dock."

Mark thought, "We haven't even gotten him very close to the boat, much less in the boat. He would have to be totally beaten or he would tear up everything in it plus us." He had read once how a tarpon had jumped and landed in a boat and done $18,000 damage.

Just then the fish made another run. "Let's go, let's go," yelled his guide. "Hell, I'm into the backing."

The boat's throttle was a little different from what Mark was used to and he moved forward tentatively, which was not enough for the guide. "We're going to lose him . . . let's go."

"Screw you," Mark thought, but jammed the throttle forward, nearly tossing the guide out of the boat.

"Damn."

Mark figured that his guide thought he could whip the fish very quickly, that he had more skill. He certainly had more strength.

Hour after hour the pattern repeated itself—race after the fleeing fish, get the line back on the small reel, then grind away. At one point Eddie exclaimed, "The friggin reel is getting hot."

"It's too small for this kind of fishing."

He grunted, probably not liking to hear the criticism.

Maybe frustrated by the way Mark ran the boat, Eddie told him to cut the engine. "If he breaks off, he breaks off."

Mark said nothing. He didn't care whether the fish broke off or not. Although many times on the water, he had never been at sea with no engine running at night. Since he felt little desire to talk to his guide, he could simply listen. A sliver of moon made its way up from the horizon. It was in this silence that he began to hear all the life, and death, going on at the water's surface. Panicky flights of baitfish broke out, then scattered from their hungry pursuers. Of this fishing trip, this time was the best. Even magical.

Meanwhile, his companion continued his struggle. Mark never offered to take back the rod, because he knew if he lost the fish, he would only receive disdain from the younger man. Slowly, though, the big fish was tiring. Eddie asked him to turn on the console and running lights. For the first time he realized no crab boat or fisherman could have seen them. At the same time, the lights, small though they were, blinded him. They were now like a little bubble of light on the dark surface.

The first time Eddie brought the fish near the boat, they could tell how big he was. At least five feet long, heavy. The fish struggled away.

"The next time he comes to the boat, I'm going to have to give you the rod so I can gaff him. You don't have to do anything. Just hold the rod steady while I gaff him."

Mark could not refuse, but he knew if the fish snapped the line, the trip back to the dock would be a chilly one. He knew too that Eddie was close to exhaustion, even in the cool night.

Eddie continued to pump away at the rod and the fish, also near exhaustion, came to the boat. He handed the rod to Mark, and with the fish still thrashing about, tried to plunge the gaff into the underjaw.

"Damn it," and once more with a powerful motion he tried to stick the fish. And it broke off. After more cursing, he said, "I'm sorry, Mark. He might have been a local record."

Mark was relieved in several ways, but said, "We got to see him though. He was some fish." He knew it was small consolation.

Back at the dock, long after midnight, they were greeted by Eddie's worried wife and children. With the relief at seeing him, she started fussing. "Couldn't you have called on the radio? I've already called the Coast Guard."

"Can you wait on all this till we get home?" he answered, annoyed.

There was no more talking and Mark collapsed in his room. The next morning as he checked out of the marina he learned that Eddie had not met his next clients. He was too beaten up. Tired as he was himself, he drove north. The farther away he got, some of his anger at Eddie passed, replaced by some sympathy for the bruising struggle the younger man had lost. His first thoughts had been "Why can't he just take this as a game, as something people played at? Why get so serious?"

Farther down the road he thought maybe Eddie's way was the better one. It was true that no one was going to use the tarpon for food, at least not in Florida. Eddie though had grown up fishing for a living, whether for stone crab or otherwise. This was the old way. Mark was the one who was infected with the modern way. The mangroves were something to get pleasure from, a background for reflection or day-dreaming. Fishing trips were little moments of pleasure. Like the trajectory of sex which led to generation in the old way, but now were merely little moments of pleasure not going anywhere. With Eddie fishing was serious, not just an idea. He didn't stand off and survey the matter like some dream, or a show on television. He and the fish and the world were still connected.

Mark had slipped up to eighty miles an hour on the interstate and knew he must restrain himself, must travel along at the same speed as everyone else. He put the car in cruise control, moved along in line with everyone else, keeping a look out for the next fast-food chain.

Does and Old Bucks

"Jeezus you remember those knockers!"

In reply, Jimmy Dolan gave out a throaty series of grunts straight from the Johnny Weismuller Tarzan movies. He could also do the best imitation of Curly from the Three Stooges that Adam had ever heard. The three men at the hunting camp had spent all their boyhood Saturdays at the Louisiana Theater on Third Street watching the serials—the Lone Ranger, Captain Midnight, Lash LaRue—only to stumble out bleary-eyed in the late-afternoon Southern heat.

"What about Jo Ann?"

"Jeezus she was a hot potato."

"Christ, she was so common, man. I mean, she had a tattoo." This was in '49 when no girl, decent or otherwise, had a tattoo.

"Hey, 'member Mary Lou? She let Dolan feel her tits during science movies."

"She didn't," insisted Ralph.

"You weren't ever supposed to tell," laughed Dolan.

"Hey, this is history," said Adam. "I'll tell you a story." When he had gotten out of the Army after three years, he came home and felt that lostness that veterans feel. After all the bars overseas, he felt com-pelled to go "across the river." In that odd geography created by the forbidden, the parish's laws closed the bars at midnight and on Sunday. In the adjoining parish, across the Mississippi River, the bars and nightclubs could stay open all the time. Adam had not been to the Carousel Club since high school. Within five minutes, he ran into a former schoolmate, Popeye, whose teeth had been rotting out even in junior-high school. He was part of the wild bunch back then and Adam did not run with him, but still he was a schoolmate, someone familiar. Playfully he had half-punched Popeye in the stomach and hit what was obviously a small pistol. Popeye just laughed it off. They talked about school days and Popeye motioned to the dance floor at a blonde in a tight skirt with great legs and ass who was putting on a real show with a guy.

"You remember her?" It was Mary Lou. As soon as she quit danc-ing Adam went over. She laughed at seeing him, gave him a kiss on the cheek and they danced. He had never dated her. She ran with the fast crowd like Popeye's. Adam had not been with a woman since Korea. He started to get ideas. As another guy danced with her while he and Popeye stood at the bar, Popeye remarked, "You know she's pro now?" Adam was stunned. He didn't feel like he could offer money to his old school friend.

"No kidding, a pro," said Ralph mournfully from his chair at the camp. Ralph had always been the quiet one in the group and he was even quieter now. Since Adam had been away from his hometown for many years, Dolan had told him in advance that Ralph had lost his wife. Hearing about Mary Lou seemed to send him further into the dumps.

"You remember Shorty, the night he threw the guy from Catholic High off the top of the stadium," remembered Adam.

"Yeah, yeah," laughed the other two. Shorty had been a really tough little nut. At most 4'11" he was still a scrapper, a drinker by the seventh grade and the first kid to get his front teeth knocked out.

"You know he went to college when he was thirty-five and now he teaches high school in one of those rough neighborhoods in New Orleans," said Ralph.

"No shit?"

"Strange but true."

Dolan warmed to the nostalgia and mentioned that Freddy, who had been a hoodlum, too, ended up a motorcycle cop. And Larry, the strongest halfback on the football team, works on a parish garbage truck because he had a big-time drinking problem.

"Mike O'Rourke is dead," he continued. "Heart attack."

"Jeezus," said Adam. Adam's father had taken him to buy his first shotgun, a single-barrel 20-gauge Iver Johnson, from Mike's father who worked in a hardware store around the corner from Third St. Dolan mentioned another classmate who had bought it pulling back from the Chosin Reservoir in 1950. Then Ralph threw in two more dead.

On a wide lamp table was a stuffed rattlesnake, a foot of its body reared up, its fangs extended, ready to strike. On the wall behind it were several large nude pinups from *Playboy* magazine.

"Where'd you get it?" asked Adam, motioning toward the snake.

"Just back of the cabin."

All three of them stared at the snake. Then as if the nudes had reminded them, they returned to their innocence and the subject of girls in their class. It was as though their testosterone levels were as high as when they were eighteen, as though those girls had not grown old either. Certainly it was true for Adam, for he had not seen any of them grow old. They were fixed as solidly for him as a sculpture of Venus.

As if to bring them back to life, the naming began again: Laurel and Helen, Sharon. As if to thaw them from their frozen past, to bring their youth and beauty down to earth, the men peppered their talk with slang. Some from school: "What a fox," "A mink, man, a real mink." Some of it was from the military days in the Far East— "That was Shorty's moose." Then slang from the world of those who had stayed in their hometown, married their high-school sweethearts, and gone to all the reunions. "She was a real moss, man." "You know O'Rourke was still following the split skirts until he had that heart attack."

The bawdy banter had turned them away from the subject of dead classmates, but O'Rourke's name brought it back. And what they could never have guessed as schoolmates, there would be those who had committed suicide. It was then that Adam got his shock; the husband of his first sweetheart, Diana, had killed himself. Adam did not know the man, and he had tried to put away the memory of Diana for years. Once he married, he thought he had forgot her.

Diana had been a swimmer with a strong, supple body. He dated her just before he went into the Army and had been in love the way an eighteen-year-old half boy, half man, could be. Although she and Adam had been in the same grade, she was in another class and he did not know her well. All the guys made noises of admiration when she passed in the hall or on the school grounds, but he never spoke to her. He first talked to her at a hunting and fishing club their fathers belonged to. She hunted on the annual winter deer hunts with her father.

One summer, though, Adam was fishing in the river that ran through the club land. He had taken a canoe out by himself, stopping to cast occasionally, when he rounded a bend in the narrow river and there she was, emerging from the river, naked, water streaming down her body, her long hair, wet and straight. She didn't see him at first, but eventually the silent canoe came closer and her face whipped around, not with fear but anger.

"Sorry," he said lamely. She sank back into the water and he paddled on. That evening, back at the lodge, he was dumb in love, and from then on for six months he pursued her. She took the matter as another kind of healthy sport, not rejecting him, but always seeming to be just beyond his reach, playing with him. Whatever it was she was pursuing, it wasn't him. He found out the classic G.I. way, with a "Dear John" letter overseas. It had filled him with humiliation. He had wanted somehow to hurt her, punish her. Since that was not possible from Korea, he got drunk any time he wasn't on line.

In the war he found he had a lot to put out of mind. You did whatever was necessary. But Diana had gone very deep, underneath memory. His friends from long ago had pulled her up, like a large bait on a hook.

"Yeah," said Dolan, "she married this guy she met at college. He had lots of money and they went off hunting all over the world—Africa, the whole bit. I don't think he was that keen on it himself, but he went. Then she got this bright idea she was going to be a dancer and went to New York to study, leaving the guy to tend to his law business. Not divorcing him, you know, just not living with him much. Must have been too much for him. A real bitch."

He paused, then "Never knew what happened to her after the suicide . . . I thought she was stuck up, myself. A real bitch." Dolan didn't know about Adam and Diana.

"I'm hitting the sack," yawned Ralph.

"Me too," said Dolan.

"I'll be right behind. I need to get some stuff out of the car," said Adam. Outside it was cold and the windshield of his car had already frosted over. He gathered the bag with his hunting clothes and got his rifle. With both hanging from his shoulders he closed the car door in the quiet and looked back at the lighted cabin. It stood next to the edge of a mostly oak forest. There was no fence and the grazing cattle could wander where they wished although Dolan said they never came around the cabin. They were not fed there, and then when hunting season came there was too much commotion for the herd.

Not only were there several large deer racks nailed to the wall of the porch, but higher, at the peak of the porch roof, were the horns of what must have been a huge Brahma bull pointing toward the moon like some great standard of a bull-god.

Because he had to get up much earlier than normal, Adam slept fitfully the whole night. Several times he reached for his small flashlight and aimed it at the little travel clock by his bed. Each time he was grateful he did not have to get out of the warm bed yet. Finally though, light shone under the door and he knew the two others were up.

He had stopped hunting deer for some time. Ten years ago while the freezing wind and rain pounded him on a stand, he vowed to give up this kind of hunting. He had taken up quail and pheasant because he could walk and stay warm. Or at least warmer than he could while deer hunting. Then, too, he simply did not go out when

it was especially miserable. Ritual though it might be, it was supposed to be fun. Yet here he was again, putting on his long johns and
camouflage.

Dolan was pouring hot water in the drip coffee pot and Ralph
was putting some canned biscuits in the oven. Adam poured some
milk over his dry cereal and watched the other two.

"I eat cereal every morning, too," said Dolan "This bum," motioning to Ralph, "thinks you have to have bacon and eggs and biscuits.
I've eaten cereal all my life." Ralph ignored both of them.

As Ralph put a dish or utensils on the kitchen counter, Adam
noticed Dolan picking them up, moving them out of the way. He
took a dish towel which seemed always to be ready to hand and
wiped any ring of water or crumb that might have fallen. After he
moved Ralph's biscuit pan to the stovetop, Ralph said, "Jeezus. You're
like an old woman fussing about her kitchen." Indeed, Adam
thought, Dolan was a far cry from his early days. No one but the
Corps ever taught him to pick up his clothes. Now he was almost
feminine in his neatness. Maybe they were all becoming soft, more
feminine. As Marines they would never have admitted it.

Adam continued eating his cereal and remembered when he had
started eating it religiously. In his fifties the fear of colon cancer was
all the rage. His father and mother had never had it, but in the 1990's
everyone was bombarded by news reports about all the cancers. Like
most folks, he wanted to live . . . forever if possible, but if not that, as
long as he could. Dolan, Ralph, and Adam had all smoked from the
time they were fourteen or fifteen, but he noticed none of them did
now. At fifteen you knew you weren't going to die. At sixty-five and
long before that, you knew you would.

As Dolan continued to fuss about the kitchen, Adam headed to
the bathroom for a second crap. He knew once he was up in a tree
stand he was trapped. If he climbed down to take one, the deer
wouldn't come around the rest of the morning. Once he had waded
a mile into a flooded slough duck hunting after eating a lot of spicy
food the night before. He was in terrible pain with nothing to do but
either go splashing away from the others and disturbing the hunt for
everyone in the woods, or enduring. He invented Zen concentration

that morning and managed to endure until the hunt was over. Never again. A guy in the next squad to his own in Korea had been shot while taking a crap, his bare butt furnishing just enough white in the night for him to be picked off.

Ralph knew the way to his stand in the dark, and Dolan had to lead Adam to his, before going to his own. As he followed Dolan, both with their rifles slung at their sides, Adam remembered the misery and the fear of Korean times. Even though he was young then, he was always tired and hungry, with never enough sleep.

Finally they came to a large oak. "We don't shoot anything with less than four points, but we got to have some meat for camp. Shoot a doe if you want. I can't get anyone who comes to the camp to do it."

Adam looked up at the old steps hammered into the tree. "You know, old buddy, this is real faith that these steps are going to hold me."

Dolan laughed quietly. "I know."

"You ever used this stand?"

"No," and laughed again, then moved away quietly in the dark.

What am I doing here? Adam thought. Climbing trees in the dark and the cold. Mustn't lose face, however. He knew if he fell before he got to the flat part of the stand, he'd break his back. The stand must have been thirty feet high. He knew as he climbed the steps that any one of them could give way. He never rested all his weight on one step, especially with the additional weight of his rifle and ammo. All went well, though, and he could just see the outline of the back of a seat someone had nailed to the tree for some comfort. Of course it was cracked and broken, but there was nothing he could do about it.

After sitting gingerly in the rotten seat, he got as comfortable as he could and rested his 7 mm. Spanish Mauser on a limb. His cousin, who had been in WW II, had sporterized the Mauser for him. He had cut the barrel off so it was flush with the long wooden stock, thus making it a Mannlicher in style, and had heated and curved the straight bolt so that a scope could be put on it. The safety could not be put on then. Adam had meant to have a gunsmith solve the problem, but after he quit deer hunting, he stopped thinking about it.

This meant that either no shell could be put in the chamber and thus not be ready to fire, or the bolt could be half closed with a shell inside. If a deer came by, the sound of the closing bolt could scare it out of range. As it was still dark, he left it half closed.

Waiting high in the tree among the limbs, he had lots of time to think about everything and anything. He noticed that just like when he was driving for some distance as he got older, his mind wandered over hundreds of things, while some other part of his brain continued to do the mechanical work. Or so he thought. Probably just inattentive to the outer world, he suspected, which can be fatal. Caught up in his thoughts hunting in the past he would feel a presence, and a deer would suddenly just *be there*. No sound, just appear like a ghost. That's when he really started to believe in intuition. Also the necessity of being quiet and still. A good recipe for seeing gods or ghosts or someone who wanted to kill you.

His stomach growled and he wished he had remembered to bring a thermos of coffee. Nothing to do but listen to it growl. As the faintest morning light appeared, he closed the bolt. Now he just had to remember not to nudge the trigger. As he held the smooth stock, he thought about the history built into the rifle, that likely it was in the Spanish Civil War. Then his own history was added to the gun. There was blood on the stock from a buck he had killed long ago. He remembered the animal vividly.

The plantation where he was hunting now had been in Dolan's family since before the Civil War. When he and Dolan had been children, Dolan's aunt had read all of *Two Little Confederates* to them while they sat in the shade under the oaks. They were read to so they wouldn't run around in the heat of the day. Back in town, he and Dolan also played at war on their street—Benjamin Street. They dug foxholes so they could make war, but the problem was always finding other kids to be the Germans. No one ever wanted to be Yankees or Germans.

Back of him was a sliver of the horned moon which gave almost no light. His thoughts returned to the night before, to the high talk about the girls of their youth, and the deaths of schoolmates. Sex was such a mystery then. Of course it had remained a mystery, but of a different kind. Now there was also the mystery of death. Sex and death. And a war in between.

Was that the great wheel of necessity?

He still felt the magic of the woods and as the nearby trees became a little clearer, the whole drama began again with this light before dawn. Little by little daylight came like a shy young woman slowly lifting her skirt, finally to reveal herself. He had read that some ancient peoples thought of the sun as feminine. Strange . . . even confusing.

After these many years, Adam was surprised how the talk about Diana had still been painful, still humiliating. Nothing like the pain of innocence, but pain nevertheless with a power to work through the layers and layers of what had come afterward. So the huntress had gone off to study dancing in New York. What next?

Now able to see any motion among the trees, he knew he needed to stay alert, and just as important, to remember that the bolt was closed and not to bump the trigger. The buck must have more than four points, camp rules. Does at your discretion. He felt ambivalent about shooting a doe. No rack, no relic to jog the memory. Still, the camp needed meat. A necessity.

Then a deer was there, the head hidden behind a tree. His heart began to pump and his movements became as slow as a snake while he positioned himself. No time for wandering thoughts now. Everything to the point.

She walked out and the Mauser roared.